The Darkness

Tales from a Revolution: Maine

The Darkness

Lars D. H. Hedbor

For Cormac —
Enjoy!

Lars DHHedbor

Brief Candle
Press

Cover and book design: Brief Candle Press.
Cover image: Frederick Edwin Church, "Twilight in the Wilderness," 1860.
Map reproductions courtesy of Library of Congress, Geography and Map Division, and the William M. Clements Library at the University of Michigan.
Fonts: Allegheney, Doves Type and IM FELL English.

First Brief Candle Press edition published 2016.
www.briefcandlepress.com

ISBN: 978-1-942319-18-4

Dedication

to Mom & Dad,
for encouraging me to look
up to the skies and back into our past,
in order to understand our world

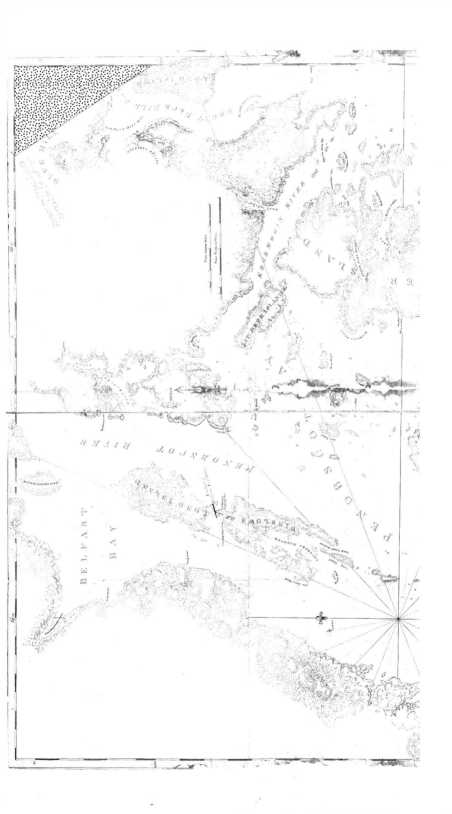

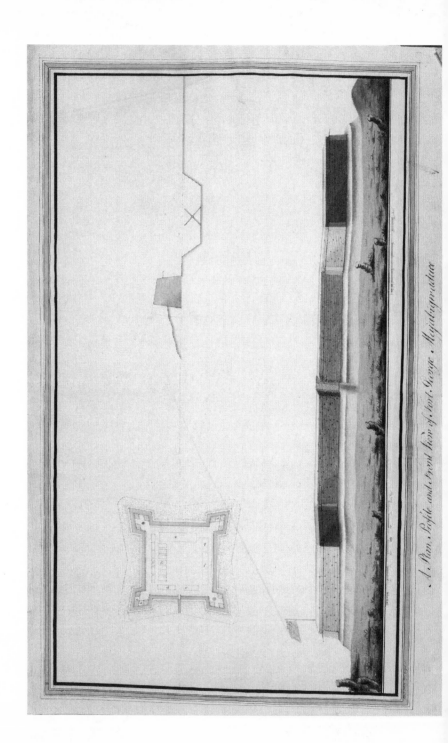

A Plan, Profile and Front View of Fort George, Megalopotaniæ

Chapter I

A shadow passed over George Williams' closed eyes and he frowned, looking to see what had interrupted him as he dozed in the warm springtime sun. He scrambled to his feet when he saw that it was his father, wearing a stern look on his face.

"Pollianne needs you," he said, and turned to leave. Stopping, he added over his shoulder, "If you were done picking stone, there was work elsewhere. Naps are for children."

George's face burned as he followed his father back toward the barn where Pollianne waited for her milking. Although he knew that there was always work elsewhere on the family's hardscrabble farm, it seemed to him that there was also time on a rare occasion for a short break from ceaseless labor.

As they crested the ridge that marked the high point along the saddle of the island that had always been home to him, George skipped his customary pause to enjoy the view, instead focusing on keeping up with the solid form of his father's strong back.

As usual, he could feel his father's disappointment and frustration as an almost physical presence. He knew that it was not all about his personal failings—just days ago he had again overheard his father describing a litany of his complaints with their situation in a late-night discussion with his mother.

"We came from Connecticut chasing the promise of good

fertile land, but it produces more stone than crops. We suffered ill enough weather where we were, but one more season like this last winter, and we'll join the Etheridges in cold graves. Colonel Campbell sits in his fort and issues commands, which we must obey or be branded as rebels. We are denied the society of our westward friends and forced to swear oaths to the King. We can scarcely buy anything, and can barely raise enough to feed ourselves and the boys. And George . . . well, he's trying."

George had cringed under his blanket at the mention of his name, but his mother interrupted his father's tirade. "Shubael, I know it's harder than we'd hoped, but we will persevere, and when this war has reached some sort of happy conclusion, we will be well-prepared to make our advantage from the restoration of peace."

She'd sighed and added, "George has always taken after me more than his brothers do, both in his appearance and in his attitude. Sometimes I wonder that you put up with me, when you rail against his faults so."

"Helen, your industry knows no limits, but George hardly knows the word. He does no more than he is asked and scarcely that, if I don't oversee him as though he were an Irish indenture." He'd snorted then. "Would that we could indenture an Irishman, but that is likely an institution that only my mother's generation will know."

George could not make out his mother's reply, but only her gentle, mollifying tone, with a final discontented rumble from his father before they both quieted and the household drifted into the peace of slumber.

Following his father now, walking briskly to keep up, George could not help but remember that the stern man ahead of him would be happy to replace him with a stranger from across the sea, only for the greater industry he would enjoy.

Scowling, he pictured this theoretical Irishman, whose speech he knew would be impenetrable to civilized ears, whose hair would be either a dense mop of wiry black, or else an even more absurd mass of carrot-shaded grease. And if his father thought that he ate prodigious quantities of potatoes, why, he'd never seen an Irishman tuck in, leaving naught for anyone else at the table.

So lost was he in his growing distaste for a person he had never met, George did not see his father stop until he'd practically run into the man.

"Did you not hear me, George?"

"Nay, I was . . . thinking."

His father scowled in disapproval at such a fruitless pursuit and repeated himself. "When you're done tending to Pollianne, bring in the rest of the herd for the evening."

"Aye, I shall, Father."

"See you do." With that, his father turned toward the house and stomped back inside.

George trudged toward the barn, hoping that he might find a moment's respite there as he fed and milked the cow.

As he entered the dim coolness, though, he heard his brothers in the loft, laughing as they moved the remainder of last season's hay from where it was stored overhead to make room for the summer haying to come.

"Hush now, Alex, here comes George."

"Ah, he won't hear us anyhow, what with how distracted he always is, Hiram."

Nonetheless, they dropped their voices to whispers so that

George could not make out what they were saying, even if he had chosen to pay attention. He was aware, however, of their presence above him, and so worked methodically through the tasks, repeating under his breath the instructions that his father had repeated to him what had seemed like a thousand times.

Give her grain to occupy her. Beside the door to the barn, George pulled aside the heavy top of the grain barrel and scooped out a generous portion, which he poured out in front of where the cow stood. She dipped her head and eagerly scooped up a mouthful and settled down to the business of chewing the treat.

Tie her securely. Looping the hempen rope around the animal's neck as he'd been shown, George knotted it with practiced fingers, murmuring comforting nonsense to her as he did. Then he slipped the other end of it around the post at the side of the barn where she stood and pulled the slack out of it. Even though Pollianne was a reliably sedate milker, his father had imposed this rule, explaining did not want George to have to chase her around the barn if something did startle her.

Always approach from the right side. He retrieved the bucket from its peg and the stool from under it, and walked down the cow's right flank, his hand trailing along her side so that his touch would not surprise her when he sat down.

Place the bucket securely. George set the stool down just in front of Pollianne's hind leg, and slid the bucket underneath her, scooting it back and forth to ensure that it was solidly set on the planks of the barn floor.

Sit comfortable. He sat down, maintaining contact with her flank as he slid his hand down toward her teat, moving the stool a bit so that he could sit on it without cramping up while he worked.

Start the flow gently. As his hand reached her udder, he sighed in frustration with himself, as he found it taut, which told him that his father was completely justified in being angry with him for being late to tend to the cow. He slid his hand down the length of the teats, squeezing slightly as he moved. His efforts were rewarded with the first warm stream of milk into the bucket, and he smiled slightly as the sweet aroma of the fresh milk reached his nose, replacing the earthier odors that usually prevailed in the barn.

Use your whole hand, and never pull. Now that her flow was started, he shifted almost without thinking about it to applying pressure with his fingers in a rippling motion, from top to bottom, over and over again. Each ripple resulted in a fresh squirt of warm milk, and he permitted himself to become lost in thought as the repeated motion settled into its normal routine.

Springtime milk, sweet with the first shoots of new grass, was perfect for butter and he knew that his mother would also set some aside for a good cheese or two, a welcome treat in the dark and cold of the winter.

As his hands moved in the back-and-forth motion, milking first one teat and then the other, he leaned into Pollianne's solid warmth, the short hair of her flanks providing a soothing and convenient surface for absently scratching an itch on his forehead.

The udders started to become slack under his hand almost before he noticed that any time at all had passed, and in the reverie of repeated, familiar motion, he did not notice when his brothers' whispering stopped.

It wasn't until Pollianne looked up sharply that he even

noticed that they had come down from the loft. Hiram popped his head down beside the bucket, saying in a teasing tone, "I bet you can't give me a shot right in the mouth."

Both George and the cow started at his voice and sudden appearance, and as she shifted around, he lost his grip on her teats. He scowled at his brother as he reached to restore his hands to their right position to finish the milking, and then started again as Alexander spoke from behind him.

"Hiram, he's lucky to even get it into the bucket, and your mouth isn't quite as wide as that."

Pollianne shifted her weight suddenly at the new sound, pushing into George and knocking him off-balance on his stool. Before he knew what was happening, he found himself on his back, looking up at Alexander's leering face.

Worse, he heard the milk in the bucket sloshing as Hiram called out, "I'll just take it from here, then, since he can't even keep his seating, much less manage poor old Pollianne."

Scrambling to right the stool, George rolled onto his hands and knees to glare under the cow's belly at Hiram as he said in a low, urgent tone, "You two know better than to disturb Pollianne while I'm tending to her. Put the milk down and get out of here."

"What, are you worried about this old beast?" Alexander reached over George to slap the cow's rump. "Don't you know that Father gave you the job of milking her because he knew that even you couldn't get on her nerves?"

While George may not have been able to make Pollianne nervous, Alexander was definitely upsetting her. She looked over her shoulder at the older boy, the whites of her eyes showing, and she shifted her weight again.

He could see what was coming, but George was powerless to prevent or avoid it. He saw the cow's leg tense up, noticed her weight coming off of it, and then watched her foot fly off the floor to catch Hiram squarely in the middle of his forehead.

George didn't know which was more distressing, the solid thud of his oldest brother's head striking the floor as he fell, or the splash of milk that filled his eyes, nostrils, and mouth, leaving him blinded and choking for breath. What he did know, though, was that his father would find some way to hold him at fault for this disaster, and his wrath would be terrible indeed.

Chapter 2

A voice rang out into the barn, while George was still mopping the spilled milk out of his eyes and regaining his breath.

"Hiram! Alexander! What mischief have you now committed, and at what cost? Our father will be little forgiving of your antics when they result in such destruction."

Alexander sputtered, "Lemuel! What brings you here at this moment?"

Stepping through the entrance of the barn, their eldest brother was at first just a dark shape against the brightness of the spring afternoon outside, but as he came closer, his three younger brothers could see that his expression carried a mixture of amusement and irritation.

Beside George, Alexander scrambled to his feet, while Hiram was slower to stand, rubbing his forehead where an angry red mark marked the point at which Pollianne had struck him. Already, a knot was beginning to rise under the spot, and George couldn't help but feel an instant of satisfaction at his brother's headache to come. Pollianne, for her part, stood placidly again, more interested in locating any last remaining grain than in the brothers' actions.

"I came to relay to our father some intelligence that I have gathered in my last visit to the fort at Bagaduce. The good colonel"—his tone grew sardonic—"claims that he has received word of a new threat from the rebels, and so wishes us to take additional steps to ensure the security of our situation here."

He surveyed the milk, now soaking into the unfinished timbers of the barn floor and turned to leave, adding, "Your immediate concern, however, must be for this mess and how you are to explain to our father that there will be no fresh milk today."

George shot a glare at Hiram, sparing a moment to share it also with Alexander and bent to pick up the bucket. Peering hopefully into it, he shook his head as he confirmed that every drop that Pollianne had given was gone to waste.

Hiram and Alexander conferred in low tones as they followed Lemuel out of the barn, and George carried the bucket over to the water barrel, dipping a bit of water into it. He gave it a swirl to rinse it out as he walked back to the barn door, and then tossed the water out into the dust, again shaking his head in irritation at the lost milk.

When he entered the house, Hiram and Alexander were nowhere to be seen, and his father's expression was not enraged at seeing him, but rather drawn and weary-looking. He barely acknowledged George's arrival, though, as he was deep in conversation with his eldest son.

Lemuel was just saying, "I believe, Father, that the colonel is again imagining things. I do not believe that the Americans would be so foolhardy as to attempt a second expedition against these parts, when their last ended in such ignominious defeat."

"We might have prevailed, but for the arrival of the British fleet." Their father made a sour noise in the back of his throat and continued, "That accursed sixty-four gun ship could not be answered, though."

Lemuel shook his head. "The British forces had built up their fortifications too much for the rebels to overcome them, even from the high ground they occupied. In any event, the British made it clear enough that they will hold this country against the Americans at any cost, and I do not believe that the General Court at Boston will again hazard ships or troops to contest the matter."

He frowned. "Colonel Campbell must also know this, yet he uses the possibility of a fresh attack to justify greater levies and more restraint over those who are unhappy enough to have fallen under his control."

His father grunted and said, "That's how war always is." He waved his hand dismissively. "I signed his loyalty oath, but I'll take my own counsel on which of his proclamations I'll follow. Don't you worry on it."

With that, the conversation was over, and their father motioned for George to come forth. As he stepped into the room, George could feel his palms go cold with the moisture that sprang from his skin.

"Lemuel says that you and your brothers wasted your milking."

Lemuel interjected, "Father, it wasn't George—" He chopped off his words as their father raised his hand in a sharp gesture that demanded silence.

"It's not your affair, Lemuel."

"Aye, Father." Lemuel gave George a veiled look and withdrew from the room.

George stood nervously as his father looked him over. He was keenly aware that he still had milk in his hair, and he could smell that his clothes were already beginning to reek of its spoiled sourness.

"You can't let your brothers do this, George." His tone was not angry—indeed, George was surprised to hear that it was almost tender. "They possess advantages over you. They are older, wiser, faster than you. Don't give them opportunities to abuse you so."

George was amazed to hear his father sigh, and to realize that it wasn't in frustration with him this time. "I've spoken to Hiram and Alexander. Get changed and go clean up. There will be more milk tomorrow. The herd still needs to come in tonight." George turned and left, feeling confused at his father's apparent transformation.

Outside, Lemuel waited for him. "I hope he wasn't too hard on you, George."

George shook his head. "Nay, indeed, he seems a changed man."

Lemuel nodded slowly, a distant expression in his eyes. "I'm not much surprised," he said, finally. "In addition to word from the colonel, I brought news to him that might cause any father to look at all his sons with fresh eyes. An old friend just buried a son—and no father can think long on that without reflecting on his own sons."

George looked at his brother sharply. "Was it anyone we knew?"

"Nay, they still live in Boston, and the son had joined up with the Continentals. The Army's been on short rations all year, they say, and the son succumbed to illness this month past." Lemuel sighed. "'Tis no way for any man to die, no matter his convictions. Why, I would offer succor even to the men of the fort across the bay there, rather than leave them to starvation and disease."

He frowned at his younger brother, adding, "Do not tell our father that I said such a thing, though, as I believe that he would welcome such hunger and privation to the enemy's camps, if it helped to bring low the King's forces in these colonies."

George looked at his brother with wonder. "I thought that Father had sworn loyalty to the Crown and to his lawful authority in these parts. Does he yet have space in his heart for outward loyalty and inward opposition to the King?"

Lemuel looked fondly at George. "Many men do, brother, or the obverse—professions of loyalty to the rebels when it is convenient, and private affection toward the Crown. This war will, in time, make liars of us all."

Ruffling a dry part of George's hair, Lemuel said, "I believe that Father would want you to clean up, yes? Best get to that before this dries onto you. I must return home to Beatrice before sundown, but I'll be back around within a few days, I'm sure."

George's head was spinning at the revelations of his father's concern for him, and the unsuspected division within his mind. The world of adult loyalties was more complex and difficult to navigate than he had ever heretofore suspected, and he was, not for the last time, glad for the relative simplicity of youth, whose largest concern could be for a spilled pail of milk.

For the next several days, George simply avoided Hiram and Alexander as much as possible. As he'd brought in the herd that afternoon, he saw that they'd been given the unenviable job of clearing out the pig pens, an assignment that their father reserved as punishment for the most serious infractions. They would doubtless be looking for revenge.

Chapter 3

At the breakfast table the morning after the milk pail incident, Hiram had feigned deafness when George had asked him to pass the cider, and Alexander had attempted to trip George with a leg strategically stuck out under a corner of the table. After that, George kept his distance, and their mother ensured that things on the table were within everyone's reach without comment.

Going about the normal routines of the farmstead in springtime, the brothers did not often need to work in close harmony, and their father, perhaps coincidentally, gave them tasks that kept them on separate areas of the farm. Alexander was in the orchards, clearing up the downed branches from winter, Hiram was in the workshop repairing the plough in preparation for turning over the fields, and George was back to picking out the stones that had risen to the surface over the winter.

By the end of each day, all three brothers were too exhausted to do more than give each other the occasional glare, and by the time Lemuel visited again, the incident had faded from their memories nearly as much as the goose egg on Hiram's forehead had receded.

Lemuel had arrived by boat this time, rowing across the bay from the mainland and pulling his shallow bateau ashore behind him, high enough to avoid the rising tide. He strode purposefully up to the barn, where George was helping their father with oiling the tack for the plough team.

"What is it, son?"

"The quartermaster has issued a new requisition of all residents of the area from the fort at Bagaduce. We are to provide, according to our acreage, certain supplies to his garrison, for which we will be paid at rates of his choosing."

Shubael answered, "He shall have them if I can supply them. We'll not quarrel with the colonel or his guns."

Lemuel nodded, handing over a note. "Here are the items he requires of your farm. I can assist you in slaughtering the pig, and will help you to load the cider."

George saw his father's face tighten at the mention of a pig, but saw an unfamiliar twinkle in his eye when Lemuel mentioned the cider.

"The pig I'd rather not part with, but I've cider suitable to his command."

Lemuel caught the look in his father's eye as well, and asked with a smile, "Did you have a barrel go poorly?"

"I would not say that it went poorly so much as it makes for a fine old vinegar."

Lemuel shook his head, the corners of his mouth still quirking upward in a half-smile. "He'll suspect you of defying his commands."

"So far as he need know, we had a bad year with all our cider."

"Aye, but he will still suspect."

"Let him suspect. His presence here should be as uncomfortable for him as it is for us."

Lemuel nodded, more serious now. "I cannot disagree."

Then he smiled widely again. "If nothing else, his quartermaster can always use the cider to cook his pork."

Shubael smiled in reply. "Your mother would add some cabbage." His smile faded and he added, "George, go tell Alexander to bring in one of the old hogs." He looked back at Lemuel. "You're certain the quartermaster wants us to do the slaughtering?"

"Aye, the order specifies that it be dressed."

"Good enough, then. Your mother will be glad for the black pudding."

George turned to get Alexander, and paused long enough to interject, "As will I!"

His brother smiled at him, while his father nodded indulgently and motioned for him to go. Though he gathered from things he'd heard his parents say that the farm could little afford to part with any animal raised for meat, George found himself salivating anyway at the prospect of his favorite sausage, and he hurried to find Alexander.

Alexander looked up from the fence he was mending when George called to him. "Why are you hollering at me like there's a house afire?"

"Father needs you to pick out a hog for slaughter and bring it up to the barn. The British have ordered us to sell them one."

Alexander looked startled for a moment, and then a slow smile spread across his face. "I know just the one, tried to knock me into the muck the other day when Father sent us into the pen." He scowled in his brother's direction at the memory, but George looked steadily back at him, refusing to be cowed.

Alexander looked away and then said, "It's the one with the black face and one white ear."

George nodded and said, "Yup, he's a mean one. Let's fetch him. Father is waiting at the slaughtering table."

"Did you bring a rope to lead him?"

George pursed his lips and said, "No, I did not. I'll go and fetch one."

"While you do that, I'll find the hog we need. Meet me in the pen."

George nodded and headed back to the barn at a trot. His father was there, already stoking the fire under a large kettle of water, and Lemuel was just getting back with another pair of bucketsful to add to it. Just inside the barn, Hiram was stropping the sticking knife, and stopped for a moment to test the edge on the hairs of his forearm.

"I forgot to bring rope to Alexander," George explained, and all three nodded at him in unison, a sight that would have been comical but for the serious expressions on all three of their faces. Hog slaughtering was not an occasion for much humor.

George retrieved the rope and carried it out to Alexander, who had already separated the hog he wanted from the rest of the pigs, and was scratching it behind the ear to calm it. George handed him the rope and took over scratching the animal's head while his brother tied the rope with a simple slipknot and looped it around the pig's neck.

George helped him draw it tight, scratching and murmuring to the pig the whole time. Alexander pulled the rope taut, and George stood up and patted the hog on the hindquarters to get it into motion.

For all that Alexander had accused it of having a mean streak a few days prior, the hog was docile enough today, and it followed without incident until they were nearly at the barn where Shubael and his other two sons waited. There, the animal seemed to pick up the scent of previous slaughtering days, and began to toss its head nervously, though it continued walking.

George could swear that the hog looked him in the eye accusingly for a moment before it planted its feet in the dirt and would not be moved further. Alexander slapped it on the rump again, though, and it grudgingly took the final few steps to stand beside the table.

There, Hiram handed the knife to his father, who said, "Hold him still. George, keep the catch basin in place."

George took the heavy cast iron kettle from the table, while his brothers positioned themselves beside the hog. Shubael looked around at them and asked, "Ready?" All four of his sons nodded, and he said, "Let us get this over with, then."

Alexander and Lemuel grabbed the animal's front and back feet and pulled them out from under it, while Hiram threw himself over the hog's flanks to hold it down. While it was still squealing in surprise and indignation, their father stuck the pig with a practiced stroke, and all five of them winced as the hog's cries took on a new, more panicked note for a few more breaths, and then fell silent.

George held the bowl steady throughout, as the pig's struggles died down, and watched in disturbed fascination as its scarlet blood pumped out in steady gouts, most of it landing in the kettle. When the flow slowed to a trickle, his father said to him, "It's done. Take that inside to your mother, and come back to help with the rest."

George was glad enough to leave the grisly scene, but he could not help but notice the warmth and fresh, metallic smell of the burden he carried. It made him feel slightly queasy and, for the moment, he could not summon his prior enthusiasm for the meal to come. In the kitchen, his mother was already measuring out the oats and herbs, and gave George a small, tight smile as he entered, panting, with the kettle.

"It never becomes any easier to see that part, George," she said as she saw the look of distress on his face. "Be glad, though, that it bothers you, for that sets you apart from those who kill without feeling or regret."

George hung the kettle on the hook she indicated on the chimney crane, ready to swivel over the fire when she was done blending in the other ingredients for the sausage. "I am not sad for the hog, Mother, as I know that we raised it for this purpose, though we hoped that more of it than this would find its way to our table."

He shrugged. "I will not deny that it disturbs me to ponder how swiftly life can leave, that with just one cut, a mortal wound may be dealt, and the last breaths drawn." He looked at his mother steadily and added, "I do not relish it, but neither will it haunt my dreams tonight."

He knew that he was not speaking the whole truth in that, but his mother nodded and said, "It is true that this is part of life on a farm. It is not altogether a bad thing that we know that meat does not come neatly hung in the butcher's window, but instead must be provided through blood and gore." She shuddered slightly. "I do not like to hear pigs scream so when it is their time, but I cannot begrudge any creature the opportunity to object to its fate in the end."

George gave his mother a smile and said, "Father and my

brothers still need my help, so I'd best get back out to the barn."

"Aye, and I need to get the sausage started before that starts to set up too much. Bring me the casings when they're ready."

"Certainly, Mother, and thank you."

She smiled as he went back outside, and she turned to begin blending the oats in, stirring and judging the proportions with a practiced eye.

At the barn, the men had completed the heavy work of hanging the carcass up by its hocks by a rope that led over a beam above the steaming kettle, its hind legs held shoulder-width apart with a stout length of wood, drilled to loop the rope through. They were just preparing to lower its forequarters into the water. Alexander and Lemuel had the rope held taut, while their father guided the hog's head into the kettle.

"Down, now. Some more. Just a bit . . . there. Now tie it off."

Lemuel looped the rope firmly over a pair of spikes on the post beside him, and then tied it off, holding it in place. He and Alexander were both panting heavily from the hard work of hauling the carcass into the air, and he bent down to catch his breath, resting his elbows on his thighs as he did so.

He arose to slap his brother on the back, a huge grin on his face. "Well done, Alexander. He was a big one, wasn't he?" Alexander, for his part, did not answer immediately, but leaned against the post, still breathing hard, a satisfied look on his face as he looked to his father for approval.

Shubael nodded to his sons. "I am glad for your help, boys." He reached into the water, twisting a tuft of hair from the hog's back to judge its readiness for scraping. "Now, get ready to lift him out. George, Hiram, come help me move him over to the table."

George and his brother came over to stand beside their father, as their older brothers unwound the rope and took up the load again. Shubael nodded to them, and they lifted the carcass out of the water.

George and Hiram helped their father swing the hog over to the butchering table, and guided it to lie on one side. As the carcass settled onto the table, he said, "Hold him there, until I say to turn him." The two brothers took hold of the pig and held it steady as their father began scraping it.

He took up the bell scraper and set to work, holding it at an angle and stripping the bristly hair from the head, and then the feet, taking care to avoid scraping through the skin. His father continued working his way up the pig's legs, and then onto its torso, up to the line where the carcass had been in the hot water.

The brothers rolled the hog to its other side when Shubael told them to, and once he'd completed the initial scraping, he used a dipper to pour more hot water over the areas he'd scraped, carrying away the loose bristles and dirt.

Then he placed the scraper flat on the pig's skin and began working it in a circular motion against the surface, scrubbing out the dirt and even the color from the skin. George was always fascinated to see how the process left the hog looking as though he had always been white-skinned, no matter how dark it had been in life.

By the time the hog's forequarters were completely scraped, even Shubael was winded, and his face shining with sweat from his exertions. After he looped the rope around its front feet, tying it off firmly, he stood aside to let his sons handle the task of submerging the hog's hindquarters in the water.

After the whole process was completed from head to tail, and the last tough patches sliced off with the sticking knife, Alexander and Lemuel again lifted the carcass to hang freely from the beam overhead, and Lemuel tied the rope off firmly to hold it in place as they gutted the animal.

"Hiram, fetch the offal cloth," Shubael instructed his son. Once the coarse cloth was in place under the carcass, he began slicing the back of the pig's neck, working his way around the jawbone, and cutting through the gullet and windpipe. Once the hog's head was free, he handed it to George, who set it on the table, reaching over after a moment and closing the one eyelid that remained open.

The remainder of the process went quickly, and soon enough, Shubael was trussing up the carcass for Lemuel to load onto his boat, and George was cleaning the intestines for his mother to use as sausage casings. He wrinkled up his nose at the smell, but knew that it was necessary for a good black pudding—and that made all the hard work worthwhile.

Chapter 4

George rubbed his hands together in an effort to warm them in the morning chill. The past season of snow and ice seemed to be grudgingly releasing its hold on the island, and he'd heard his parents comment on multiple occasions during the dark months that it had been the hardest winter they could remember. He was waiting by the shoreline for Lemuel, who was to bring him to town for the day, with a list of items his mother desired him to purchase for the coming season.

The sun had risen now, with the promise of warmth later in the day, but a dense line of trees stood along the ridge above the beach where his brother was to meet him, and in their shadow, it was still cold enough that he could see his breath.

He could hear a rooster crowing from somewhere behind him, announcing that daybreak had come to his part of the island, and in the distance, he could hear a hound of some sort howling mournfully. It was probably Lemuel's dog, bereft at being left behind while its master went off on some errand without him.

Just then, the prow of Lemuel's boat swung into view around the entrance to the cove, and George called out to him.

"Hullo, Lemuel!"

"Good morning to you, George!" Lemuel's voice carried cheerfully across the cold water. As he drew closer, he said, "You have Mother's list?"

"Yes, naturally, and the money that Father provided to pay for what she requires."

Lemuel strained at the oars for a few more strokes, and as the boat scraped onto the shore, he said, panting, "Then I pray that we will be able to secure the items we need. Come, jump aboard."

George stepped onto the boat with one foot and pushed it off with the other before scrambling into his seat beside Lemuel as the boat drifted silently into the cove. Both took a moment to adjust the oars so that they were placed for two oarsmen instead of one, and at a nod from Lemuel, they began pulling in unison.

Their labor precluded much conversation, until they emerged from the lee of the island and the prevailing breeze could reach them. The sight of the sail rising under Lemuel's experienced hands and then filling with wind to hurry them on their way made George's heart glad, and Lemuel's quiet assurance as he adjusted the sail and set the tiller into the water that sluiced by the side of the boat filled him with admiration. He wondered whether he might ever gain the ability to conduct himself on the water with such skill.

Lemuel did not ask for his help, and George did not offer it—it was a simple craft, designed to be sailed by one person, and George knew from experience that extra hands would only confuse the process of managing the sail and tiller.

This left George free to ponder the shoreline as they approached, marred as it was by the unwelcome intrusion of the fortifications that the British had thrown up upon seizing this area the prior year.

It had mushroomed, seemingly overnight, from a set of rude trenches and earthworks, to fully-realized fort, with low-slung timber walls punctuated with high blockhouses at each corner. The whole affair crouched, sullen and ominous over the town as a silent threat, and the British flag on its staff served as a daily rebuke to all those who wished that the King would tend to his own affairs and leave this small settlement in peace.

Lemuel steered the boat around the peninsula on which the fort stood, and as they passed into the shadow of the structure, the chill of the morning reasserted itself. They emerged back into the sun as they sailed past the narrow neck of land that connected it to the mainland, which was interrupted with additional walls and defenses. Lemuel furled the sail as they approached the land, calling out to George, "Get ready on the oars, now."

George centered himself between them, and as Lemuel managed the tiller, he began pulling at the oars to keep their momentum toward shore going.

His brother picked the spot on the shore where he wanted to land the boat, and said, "Just a bit more, George . . . good, you can stop rowing now."

The gravel of the beach grated underneath the boat, and George laid the oars back along the sides of the boat and stood, stepping over the side of the prow to drag it further ashore. Lemuel joined him, and the two brothers pulled the small craft well out of reach of the waves.

"Tide's going out soon, and we'll be back before it comes up this far again," Lemuel said, and George nodded in reply. "Shall we go to the mercantile together, and then attend to the rest of our errands individually?"

"That suits my purposes," George answered, and they set off.

The village was relatively quiet, but a few townspeople were in evidence, going about their daily affairs with friendly smiles and familiar nods to the two young men.

They reached the mercantile, and they each in turn presented their shopping lists to Mr. Jones, who had bought out the prior owner of the shop with the arrival of the British. Mr. Rutherford, who had sold it, was said to have joined up with the rebels at Machias, further up the coast, where the Americans had a stronghold.

Jones didn't go for all that political intrigue, and was well satisfied to do business with all comers, British and Americans alike. Some of the rebel sympathizers in town avoided his store, but like most people, George and Lemuel gritted their teeth and bought what they needed from him.

George's pile of goods was quite a bit heftier than Lemuel's when they were finished, but he gathered it all into a sack and said, "Mr. Jones, I trust that we may leave these with you for safekeeping, until we have finished with my other business in town and we are ready to return home?"

"Of course," said the merchant, a knowing smile on his face. "Can't leave goods unattended these days, what with all the lawlessness and disruption lately in these parts."

Lemuel smiled in reply, perhaps a bit cooler than Jones, and said, "Indeed, with our visitors about, any peculiar thing could happen to unguarded valuables."

The other man's smile stiffened a touch, and he nodded politely. "I'll keep them under my personal observation until you are ready to collect them."

George nodded to him, and as the brothers left the mercantile, he hissed at Lemuel, "Why did you prod him so?"

Lemuel gave George a grim look and said, "I'll not make the British occupation of this district any more easy than it absolutely must be. They are interlopers in this colony, and those who sympathize with them, too. I mean to make him uncomfortable."

"You'll be reported as a rebel supporter."

"Nay, I am most careful to not give them cause to act." He shrugged. "And if he reports me, let him. They'll find nothing in examining me."

"Or Beatrice?"

Lemuel's face grew stormy. "They'll leave my wife out of it entirely, if they have any care for their skins."

"'Tis your skin at risk, more than theirs." George motioned up the hill at the fort. "One man can hardly argue with that."

Lemuel gave George a stubborn grimace, but he did not answer, instead pausing for a moment before saying, "I'll meet you back here at around noontime."

George nodded and said, "I'll keep an eye on the sun." Without another word, the brothers parted, Lemuel to attend to some business he'd not chosen to elaborate upon, and George to see about making arrangements to trade with a local trapper.

He entered a narrow alley between two houses, a shortcut he preferred over walking the long way around the long line of houses and businesses. As he entered the shadowed space where the eaves from the two buildings nearly met, he heard a girlish shriek, followed by what sounded like a hand striking bare flesh and a grunt of surprise.

Cautiously, George proceeded toward the source of the noise, feeling his heartbeat pound in his ears. Coming around the corner in a crouch, he saw a young woman standing over the writhing form in the uniform of a British soldier.

She was facing away from George and had not heard his approach, and he was surprised to see her draw her foot back and kick the soldier on the chin, saying in a low, angry voice, "That'll serve you for thinking that you can just take of any colonial girl whom you fancy." George wasn't sure, but he thought he heard the crack of bone breaking when her boot struck the man's face.

He had no time to wonder, though, as the girl turned to leave and caught sight of him. She gave out another small shriek and covered her mouth in surprise, her eyes narrowing in anger.

"Are you in league with this devil, then?" she asked, advancing on George with a menacing manner.

Despite himself, he found that he was frightened for his safety—this was obviously someone to reckon with. "Nay, I just heard your exclamation a moment ago, and came to see whether you needed any assistance." He gestured at the now-still figure on the ground behind her and added, "I can see now that you do not."

Her posture softened, and shoulders sagged as she said, "Thank God. I did not relish fighting off another." She approached, looking smaller and more vulnerable than she had a moment before, and George could see that she was shaking visibly.

He felt the urge to take her into a comforting embrace, but stifled that impulse, saying, "We had best be elsewhere when he awakes. I think you broke his jaw, and the garrison here will not look kindly on one of their own being so injured in town, no matter the circumstances." She gasped slightly and took his elbow in her hand, guiding him around the far corner of the building he'd just passed by. "Come quickly, then, and let us tell my father what has happened. He will know what to do."

Though he had no part in her predicament, George felt moved to help her if he could, and followed at a jog behind her as she pointed the way through the maze of houses in the village center. They emerged back onto the main road, and she released his elbow, slowing to a more normal pace, as there were more people moving about than had been earlier in the day.

A patrol of four British soldiers was among those on the street, and for an instant, George felt as though his heart had stopped in his chest. The girl spotted them, too, and turned as casually as she could to George, leaned in toward him, and said in an urgent whisper, "Kiss my cheek."

George tried to hide his startled expression, as he realized what she was trying to do, and mustered the courage to give her a quick, chaste buss. Though the kiss might have been faked, the blush that spread over his face afterward was completely authentic.

The brief contact between his lips and the petal-soft skin of her face lasted for only the briefest of instants, and yet it seemed as though the entire morning ran its course before the connection between them ended.

Acting her role a bit too convincingly, the girl gave him a coquettish little smile and turned away, her skirts swirling about her feet as she strode away. He hazarded a glance up and down the street, and was somehow shocked to find that nobody else present—including the bored soldiers—seemed to have noticed the moment at all.

Shaking his head to clear his thoughts, George willed his breathing to slow, even as he could feel his cheeks still burning, and turned away from the patrol to find a more roundabout path to his meeting with the trapper.

As he walked down the road with his ears abuzz, he shook his head at the knowledge that he didn't know where the girl had gone to seek refuge with her father. Indeed, although the warmth of her cheek was etched into his memory, he realized that he hadn't even learned her name.

Chapter 5

On the trip back to the island, George was lost in thought, and Lemuel had to ask him three times to stow the oars as he raised the sail. For his part, Lemuel did not seem all that inclined to make unnecessary conversation either, and together the two of them passed back under the forbidding face of the British fort and across the bay, keeping company with only their own thoughts.

Lemuel beached the boat in the cove and George helped him push it back off, shouldering the sack of goods from the mercantile as he waved his farewell. He trudged back up to the house, still replaying the events of the morning in his mind.

Entering the house, he brought the sack into the kitchen, deposited it on the table and tore a chunk off of a loaf of bread he found there. His mother looked around from the pot she was tending and said, "Did you and Lemuel get all that you needed in town?"

"Aye, Mother, everything on the list. Mister Jones' prices seem to have gone up again, but what with the sale of that hog to the quartermaster, we had enough to pay for it all this time."

He took a bite of the bread and chewed it thoughtfully as he sorted through the sack, placing the items in it on the shelves where they belonged until they were needed. "Father wanted these nails in the barn, did he not?"

She nodded, and he set them aside to bring out when he was finished in the kitchen. He remarked, "These needles were particularly dear, but I knew that you needed them especially, what with all of the clothes that Hiram needs sewn back up this season."

She sighed and answered, "You were right to pay the price, whatever it was. I broke my last needle a week ago, trying to stitch the heel back onto his boot. I expect to be making and mending clothing for you, as you're still not fully grown, but your brother ought really know enough to avoid destroying his clothing."

George shrugged philosophically, saying nothing, but taking another bite of the bread. His mother gave him an exasperated look and took the sack away from him.

"Bring the nails to your father. I'll put the rest of this away. And if you see Hiram, tell him to come see me?"

Muffled by the mouthful of bread, George answered, "Yes, Mother," and picked up the bundle of nails. As he walked out to the barn, still lost in pleasant thoughts about the incident at the village, he encountered Hiram, who was walking with a limp, and had a fresh hole in the knee of his pants, stained crimson with the blood that trickled down his leg.

George stopped and gawped in amazement, and Hiram scowled at him. "What, have you never seen a cut knee before?"

"It is not that, Hiram. Mother is already preparing to scalp you over the shoe you ruined, and now you come in like this? What happened this time?"

Hiram's scowl grew no less fierce as he answered, "I fell over a timber laid out in the barn."

George gave Hiram a puzzled look. "Father doesn't usually

lay out work within the barn when the weather's decent."

Hiram flushed slightly and answered, "Nay, it was my own work, something Alexander and I were trying to accomplish."

George shook his head. "I don't need to know any more about your affairs. You had best go see Mother and get it over with. I know that she has needles for mending again, as I just placed them in her hands myself."

Resignedly, Hiram left without another word, and George continued on to the barn. There, he found his father chastising Alexander.

"What were you boys thinking?" He sounded more tired than angry at this point, having likely put up with the brothers' shenanigans all morning.

"Hiram wanted to try to raise the timber up to the loft, so that he could convert it into a walled-off room, instead of just open rafters with some boards laid across them."

"What in the name of—" Shubael cut off his exclamation as he saw George, but his expression remained grim. "Go and finish your chores, Alexander. I'll see you back here after they're all done to put this to right again."

Shubael's head swiveled as he watched Alexander leave the barn, and his mouth was fixed in a stern look. His expression did not soften when he swung back to fix George with his gaze.

"I trust that you and your brother managed to secure the items we needed for the season?"

"Aye, Father. Here are the nails that you had on the list."

His father reached for the bundle, and George handed them over. Shubael examined them for a moment and remarked, "The smithy Jones gets these from is trying to skimp again, I see. These have scarcely any heads knocked onto them, and I think that they're shorter than they ought be as well."

He sighed and carried them over to place them on a shelf along the wall. He asked, over his shoulder, "Did you two manage to avoid any unplanned adventures?"

George shifted uncomfortably, and his father turned around to look at him, an immediate look of suspicion on his face. "Tell me what happened, George, before I have to hear about it from some gossip, who will only make any trouble that your brother stirred up with the British sound many times worse than it even is."

"In truth, Father, I know not whether Lemuel had any trouble with anyone of the garrison, and for my part, I only happened upon an incident, one not of my making. Indeed, whatever part I may be judged to have played in it only took place in the aftermath."

Shubael now turned the full force of his attention onto George, and nodded expectantly, a grim expression forming on his face. "And what part might that have been?"

George found himself explaining the whole situation with the girl, and when he came to the part of the story where she insisted upon a kiss, he blushed anew.

His father's face relaxed, and he even cracked a smile at George's discomfiture. "She sounds like a strong-willed girl, and a fast thinker. There aren't many of your generation with the wit to escape an attack such as it sounds that she was being subjected to, much less the strength of will or limb to so thoroughly discourage their attacker."

"Won't the garrison be on the alert for her?" George's worried expression was enough to get another smile out of his father. His concern for the girl was obviously more keen than it might have been without the tiny intimacy she had shared with him.

"Nay, I doubt that he was willing to admit that he'd been bested by a girl in a fight. He'll have made up some story about having been in a bar brawl or some like, and she'll be safe from the garrison." He frowned. "I should hope, however, that he does not catch her alone in an alleyway again, for she will likely not be able to surprise him so twice—and I expect that he'll be nursing a grudge, as well as a sore jaw."

"Worse than sore, if I heard that break aright."

His father nodded. "Aye, he may be lucky enough to eat again, never mind speak clearly of how he came to be so injured."

He squared his shoulders and slapped his thighs explosively, saying, "It does sound as though your new acquaintance is a person worth knowing better, should you find yourself with that opportunity."

George blushed again, and his father shook his head, still smiling. "Well, you will if you will, and you won't if you won't. I'll not meddle in your affairs, any more than I interfered with Lemuel and his Beatrice. You're young yet, but then, when I met your mother, I was scarcely older than you are now."

George protested, "I am not interested in her beyond assuring myself that she was not molested by any in the garrison, and I am certainly not ready to marry, in any circumstance."

His father smiled knowingly, infuriating George. He whirled away from his father and left the barn, without so much as asking his leave, and he could swear that he heard a strange sound from within the barn that might even have been his father laughing.

Chapter 6

A warm spell had settled in over the island, though it was accompanied by a dismal cast to the sky. There was a hint of smoke in the air, and George wondered whether some battle of the seemingly endless war had taken place upwind somewhere. Perhaps the rebels were going to make another attempt on the fort here—and George wished only the direst of fates on the soldier who'd attacked the girl in the alley.

Though it had been weeks since the incident in town, he found his thoughts returning to her over and over again as he went through the routines of his daily chores. He did not make the mistake of discussing her with his father again, although he thought that he detected a certain new lightness in Shubael's demeanor, a small but noticeable change from his normally-dour attitude.

In particular, the memory of the girl's cheek—its smoothness and welcoming warmth, the sensation of touch—kept leaping into George's memory at the most unexpected moments. He felt certain that he would never again experience a moment that would stay with him the way that kiss was, even if it was purely strategic and unromantic for its recipient.

In any event, thinking about the girl in the alley was certainly more pleasant than focusing on the work he was doing. He picked up the handles of the sledge and groaned as he jerked it into motion behind him. Though his brothers had been rewarded for their antics with a month's worth of pigpen duties, it had fallen to George to distribute the pigs' waste onto the fields, where it could do the most good for the crops. He hauled the fully-laden sledge forward another few paces, and then set it down again, pulling the shovel out of the pile to begin tossing the dung over the freshly-turned earth.

His arms already ached from the heavy work, but when he'd complained the day before his father said, the same as a hundred times before, "Be grateful that we have this land to work on, and be grateful that your lot is easier than mine was at your age. When I was a boy, I used buckets for this job, instead of a nice solid sledge, and I went to bed hungry more often that you do, to boot."

At least there was food in the kitchen these days, and the porridge his mother had spooned out this morning had even had a bit of meat in it—Alexander had been lucky with a snare, and an unwary rabbit had found its way into the family larder the day before. Not that George's gut wasn't already grumbling and ready for something more, but at least he didn't feel lightheaded, as the labor of some days left him.

As he worked, he puzzled at the problems of what pretense he could use to get into town again, how he could find the girl, and how he could learn her name. This was both a welcome diversion from the labor, and a deep frustration, because he was not able to readily solve even the first problem, much less the second, and the third made him feel as though his stomach was turning flips within his belly—and not from hunger.

Although he most frequently revisited the moment of the kiss, George also cherished the impish, teasing, and perhaps—dared he hope?—flirtatious smile as she darted away. Too, he remembered well the strength she had exhibited in overpowering and subduing her attacker, and her willingness to take him on in turn, had his intentions been malign as well.

He finished spreading dung over the section where he had dragged the sledge, and moved the load down the row another several paces. The sky had started to look downright menacing, as dark clouds boiled up along the horizon. It looked like the afternoon was going to be a good one to spend in the barn or, better yet, indoors, perhaps even helping his mother in the kitchen.

Of the three brothers in the house, he was the only one who actually enjoyed the slicing and scraping and stirring that she asked of them, and he spent many cheerful hours in quiet conversation together with her. Hiram and Alexander were more inclined to do only the minimum that they could get away with, before sneaking off to the barn, or even out into the fields to help their father with chores that they felt were more in keeping with their place as men of the family.

They had, however, stopped teasing George for choosing to help their mother keep food on the table, after receiving a particularly sharp dressing-down from their father one afternoon when he'd caught them tying George up in an apron and demanding that he make them tea and biscuits. That evening, George and his mother had sat at leisure at the dinner table, while his two brothers attended to them like servants and their father glared silently at them.

In spite of himself, George smiled at the memory as he began lifting and spreading the pig manure across the next section of the field. Though Shubael's sternness usually did not augur to his youngest son's benefit, his deep sense of justice sometimes could go no other direction.

As George worked, the sky grew darker and darker, and as the clouds rushed to fill the last remaining open spots of sickly yellow-cast sky, the first spatter of raindrops fell, heavy and cold, onto his back. He knew that his father would not accept mere physical discomfort as an excuse, so George did not pause in his work, but he was a bit less diligent about spreading the dung evenly than he had been at the beginning.

It was dark enough now that George could hear the birds in the trees at the edge of the field singing their evening songs, though they sounded confused and forlorn. The cattle were moving of their own volition to the barn, too, just as though it was the end of the day, and not close to noontime.

After hauling the dredge forward just a few more times, he finally tossed the last shovelful onto the field, and turned the lightened load around to return it to the pigpen. The rain was coming down with stolid purpose now, though it fell in an eerie stillness, with hardly any breeze accompanying the storm.

By the time George gratefully dropped the handles of the sledge, he was soaked through to the skin, and although the rainfall had slowed somewhat, the skies continued to darken, to the point that he could see through the window of the house that his mother had lit candles in order to go about her work within.

He weighed the potential consequences of leaving his task unfinished against the very real discomfort he was enduring as the rainwater sluiced over his face and down the back of his neck. A fresh downpour convinced him that the better course was to risk his father's wrath over nature's, and he left the sledge and shovel to wash off in the storm, walking toward the house. A flash of light startled him, and the boom of thunder that followed immediately after propelled him through the door.

Closing it behind him, he was surprised to see that it was still growing darker, and he could scarcely even make out the barn across the yard in the gloom. The warmth and light of the fireplace and candles in the kitchen seemed like a far wiser choice than staying out in this strange and foreboding storm.

Helen had turned to regard her son as he came through the door, and stifled the shriek that wanted to leap from her throat at the thunderclap that accompanied him into the house. Now she stood regarding him with a mixture of concern and resignation.

Unlovely at best, with his hair now plastered across his broad features, his clothing pasted to him by the rain, and a general aroma of pigpen rising from him into the air of the kitchen, her expression reflected the difficulty of being glad to see him enter.

"You should change out of your wet things," she finally said, waving him to the stairs and handing him a candlestick for light. "Bring them back down with you, and we'll set them to dry before the fire." George nodded, and as he went up the stairs, he heard the front door open and slam closed twice more.

"It has the feel of Judgement Day without," he heard his father say.

Alexander added, "Hiram here was nearly called home to his reward early by that stroke of lightning. It split a tree not twenty paces from where he stood, and left it burning like Moses' bush."

Shubael's impatience with Alexander's hyperbole was audible in his tone as he retorted, "If you boys had been working on the task to which I set you this morning, you would have been nowhere near that ridge, and the barn would be swept out in the bargain. Go get out of those clothes, and then I will find something useful for you both to do."

The two brothers crowded up the stairs as Shubael continued, "Helen, have you seen George yet? It is unlike him to stay out long in such weather."

"He is upstairs already. Is it really so dark without that you could not see him enter just before you?"

Hiram entered the close, warm room that the brothers shared, looking too unsettled and shaken to take much note of George's presence there. He was followed immediately by Alexander, who was pleased enough to give George an excited, but silent jeering gesture.

"It is as dark as night out there, save for when the lightning struck." Shubael paused, and George could hear water falling to the floor as his father apparently wrung out some portion or another of his garments. "I have never seen the like of this weather, nor even heard old tales to match it. Between a winter that put me in mind of End Times, and now this, I should not be surprised to hear trumpets and a shout from Heaven at any moment."

"I dislike it when you talk so, Shubael," his mother chided gently. Their father answered in a quieter tone that George could not hear, and she replied, "Just get those wet things off, before you catch a chill."

In short order, all four men sat about the dinner table in whatever clothing they could find, while their outfits hung, steaming, before the fire. Hiram looked particularly absurd in a shirt that he had outgrown and passed down to George some time back, but it was all that the boys had been able to find dry. The sleeves barely came past his elbows, and the fabric of the back was tight across his shoulders.

"Have you nothing else to wear, Hiram? I know that you have a second shirt somewhere."

"I ripped the side open," he mumbled, avoiding her eyes.

She looked fully exasperated as she exclaimed, "How did you manage that?"

This time, his response was unintelligible.

His father gave him a dour look. "Answer your mother, Hiram."

"I fell out of a tree, and it caught on a branch."

George could see his mother counting to ten behind closed eyes as she drew one measured breath after another. When she opened her eyes, she simply said, "Go and fetch me the ruined garment, and I will see whether I may be able to make some repairs to it."

Shubael said, "Or you could set him to work on it himself." He gestured out at the darkness beyond the window. "We cannot work outdoors in this, so he may as well make himself useful in recompense for his foolishness."

Though it sounded as though the storm had passed, and the rain had stopped now, George still could see nothing of the outside world through the window, any more than if it were midnight, and not midday. Hiram stood and fetched a lantern from the shelf before he made his way up the stairs, still not meeting his mother's stern gaze with his eyes.

Alexander seemed lost in thought, staring blankly at the fire, his attitude substantially subdued now that the excitement of witnessing the lightning strike at close range had passed. He finally spoke. "Father?"

Shubael's eyes flicked over to where his son sat, registering surprise at Alexander's appearance. He answered, "What is it, Alexander?"

Alexander looked up now, and George was surprised to see fear in his brother's eyes. "Do you really think that this could be the End Times, as we've read about?"

Shubael's eyes narrowed as he gazed at his son, and his mouth pursed for a moment. Finally, he looked away, saying, "You should not be listening in on the conversations of your elders. There's no sense in worrying about that which is beyond our ken or control; if the Lord chooses this moment to snatch us all up for judgment, it is not for us to protest or resist."

He sighed, and looked back to meet Alexander's questioning gaze. "For whatever comfort it gives you, though this war has tried our souls, and doubtless gives our Maker much cause for sorrow, I do not see the signs that we were promised of the coming of Armageddon, and you need not worry that our Father will soon pass judgment on your youthful misdeeds."

Alexander held his father's gaze for a moment longer, and then looked down, nodding. George could not tell if he had found any comfort in his father's reassurance, but Alexander seemed at least satisfied to let the matter rest.

Hiram returned at this moment, the rent garment draped over his arm. Helen leapt up from her seat to take it from him, exclaiming, "It looks as though you tried to use it as a sail in a tempest!"

Hiram looked abashed, and looked down at his feet as he replied, "I did try to use the cloth after the shirt was ruined, to reproduce Doctor Franklin's results with his kite."

His mother's mouth sagged open in disbelief, and George had all he could do to stifle his laughter as she looked back and forth between her son and the ruins of the shirt she held up before him. Only a fresh rumble of thunder, and a return of the drumming of rain on the roof, saved Hiram from a worse tongue-lashing than he had already received, and he took advantage of his mother's glance out the window into the darkness of the day to escape back up the stairs.

She sat down in tight-lipped silence and began rejoining the shreds of fabric, shaking her head and making inaudible, but foul-toned comments to herself, while her husband and sons studiously looked away to avoid her anger turning on them.

The rain began to abate again, and Shubael said to George, "Pollianne is still going to need milking, whether it is light or not. When I passed the barn, she was already sheltering within, and I doubt that she has stirred since."

George nodded, and rose to make his way out to the barn, and though the animal's ears twitched when she saw him carrying a lantern into the dark cavern of the structure, she behaved well enough as he went through the well-practiced steps of the milking ritual. When he was finished, he gathered up the pail and gave her an extra measure of grain, patting her on the neck and murmuring, "That's a steady girl. Best just stay in the paddock, as though it were night, I think."

He pulled the doors of the barn closed behind him after he led her into the enclosure with the rest of the cattle, and then picked up the pail and his lantern to return to the house. Though there was no more rain, the smell of ashes was more pronounced than before, and he wondered what phenomenon of nature could possibly explain this sunless day, if it weren't some omen of the end of the world.

He thought that there was certainly enough wickedness afoot to tempt the Lord into just bringing it all to an end. Ranging from the large and horrid depredations of armies upon one another as they ranged about the countryside of this hopeful new nation, down to the individual acts of villainy such as the soldier who had attacked the girl in the alley, it seemed hard to reconcile Christ's promises of forgiveness and love with the world as it was in these violent days.

With this train of thought, George found himself brought full circle, back to the girl in town, and he looked in the direction of the village across the bay, wondering how she fared in this strange darkness. He saw only a few scattered sparks of light, not unlike the normal view on a winter's evening, when the people of the town tried to extend their days just a little bit with what small efforts candles and whale oil could make against the darkness of night.

And here it was, only afternoon, but near to summer, and they were all reduced to a few tiny bright spots in a world that seemed to have given up hope of seeing the sun rise again.

Chapter 7

George was sitting at the table, watching his finger trace meaningless patterns over its surface when his mother finished sewing the scraps of fabric that Hiram had presented to her back into something resembling a shirt. She held it up, *tsk*ing to herself a couple of times as she examined it. "Well," she remarked to nobody in particular, "it may never fit him again, but at least it's serviceable now."

Hiram, who had crept back downstairs, looked up, and though he still had the grace to look somewhat abashed, said, "Thank you, Mother. I will take more care to avoid damaging my clothes further."

She shot him a stern look and handed the shirt over to him. "See that you do."

She peered out the window then and said, "Shubael, I do believe that the darkness is lifting" All five members of the family went outside, looking in wonder at the strange sight of the darkness relieved not from across the bay where the sun rose, but from behind the house, to the West.

Soon enough, though, the darkness of true night reasserted itself, by which time they had retreated to the warmth and comfort of the house. Rather than waste candles on staying up discussing the same theories that they had already talked through a dozen times, trying to explain and understand the strangeness of the day,

Shubael sent the boys up to sleep, and he and Helen stayed down by the dwindling coals, keeping company quietly until weariness called them to their own bed.

The sun rose normally in the morning, and though the sky remained cloudy and unhealthful in appearance, it did not repeat its performance of the prior day, and the day progressed in its normal routine, interrupted only by Lemuel visiting around midday, checking to see that everyone had escaped unscathed through the storm.

Alexander had regained his usual ebullience, and as the boys worked on the neglected barn sweeping, he regaled his brother with the tale of the burning tree, and Hiram's close call with the forces of nature, and their mother.

Lemuel shook his head, smiling at Alexander's enthusiastic telling of the story, while Hiram kept his head down, working steadily and refusing to answer Alexander's taunts over the ill-fitting patchwork shirt he wore today.

Finally, Lemuel interrupted Alexander's retelling of the adventure of the lightning strike, saying, "I had in mind going over to town tomorrow, if either of you are free to accompany me?"

This ended Alexander's storytelling, as he said, suddenly somber, "Nay, Father has given us an unending list of tasks to attend to, since he felt that we were failing to do our part when the storm struck." He gave Lemuel a sly smile, though, and added, "I don't doubt that George should like to go back to town and try his luck with the girl in the alley again, however."

Lemuel arched an eyebrow at his brother. "Girl in the alley? I did not suspect that any son of my father would consort with such, least of all George." He frowned. "I did not suspect that our little town even had such girls, although the presence of a fort will bring out the worst, I suppose."

Alexander snorted, and Hiram interjected, "She was in distress, and to hear George tell it, is the very picture of chaste modesty." He looked downward, and added, "Not that we are supposed to have heard him tell the story."

Alexander smirked and said, "I overheard Father telling Mother about it, when she asked why George was behaving so strangely after your last trip to town. He tried to rescue this girl from a soldier who had accosted her in the alley, but she had already dispatched the ruffian, and needed only to have George kiss her so that her appearance in the street would pass unnoticed."

He frowned. "I do not fully understand why she should have chosen George to kiss, nor what made her believe that kissing such a specimen would be less of a spectacle than simply appearing alone on the street."

Shrugging, he said, "I may not have heard the story with complete clarity, but in any event, he has been pining to return to town on any excuse ever since. The only impediment is whether or not Father will release him from his chores."

Lemuel smiled and replied, "Well, then, I should ask Father. Be productive in your pursuits today, that you might sometime have the opportunity for such adventures."

Alexander favored his brother with a sour look before turning to Hiram to say, "He makes sport of our lonely suffering."

Hiram shrugged philosophically and continued sweeping, and Lemuel left the barn to look for their father. He found Shubael mending a fence that had been knocked awry in the storm, and strode across the field to greet him.

"Good day, Father—I trust that you are well despite yesterday's upsets?"

"I am," Shubael replied, and continued working, deepening the post-hole from which a worn post had fallen. He grunted slightly with each impact of his spade on the bottom of the hole, lifting sodden earth to pile alongside its rim.

"I had planned to visit town today, to learn what I could of the event, and I am given to understand that George may have a particular interest in accompanying me?"

His father set the spade against the fence and said, with an enigmatic smile on his face, "I take it that you have been sharing gossip with your brothers, whose curiosity is exceeded only by their skills at eavesdropping?"

Lemuel smiled widely and said, "The story reached me with what sounded like fantastic embellishments, but I believe that I understood enough of it that George would appreciate the opportunity to try his luck at finding a girl he knows there."

His father nodded slowly and said, "He could tell me little about the girl, save that she was resourceful and possessed of a face that would bring an angel to tears of envy." He rolled his eyes, and Lemuel chuckled. "In any event, I will not stand in the way of his pursuit of joy, so long as he does not bring dishonor on our family. I would be cautious about trusting Alexander or Hiram, but George does not worry me so much as his brothers."

He nodded again, a faraway look in his eyes. "Indeed, I worry in the main that he will be misused, and not that he would make any attempt to take advantage of a girl." He seemed to stop himself from saying more, and concluded simply, "I can spare George for the afternoon. He is up on the ridge, spreading the last of the dung."

Lemuel nodded back in acknowledgement. "I will keep my brother under my eye, then, but not so closely that he cannot find a chance to seek what fortune may await him. We will be back before nightfall."

Shubael waved and picked up the spade again, turning back to the task at hand.

When Lemuel found George, his younger brother was just finishing yet another sledge of pig leavings, and was quite enthusiastic about setting aside the work in favor of a trip over to town.

"I should like to get cleaned up first," he said, trying, but failing, to contain his enthusiasm.

"Of course," said Lemuel, a tolerant smile playing across his lips. "Only do not take very long, as we are to be home before the night."

George nodded eagerly and after he had brought the sledge back to the pig pen to await tomorrow, and the next load, he all but ran back to the house to change into cleaner clothes, followed inside at a more measured pace by his brother.

As he sped up the stairs, his mother called up from the kitchen, "George, do you not yet have work in the field that your father has asked you to complete?"

"Aye, but he told Lemuel that I might have leave to accompany him into town."

Lemuel walked into the house then, saying, "Father thought that George might like the chance to visit town again." In a quieter tone, inaudible to George as he dressed, he added, "There was something about a girl there, whom he does not wish to court, but does wish to learn more of." He did not quite wink at his mother, and she did not quite wink back as she smiled knowingly and nodded her approval.

"I see," she said aloud. "Well, I want for aught, so soon after his last trip to the mercantile, but if he should happen to see a good price on some sturdy broadcloth, it would not be an unwelcome addition."

She frowned, adding, "We shall have to sell another hog to the garrison, however, if prices keep being driven up by the convulsions in our trade." She sighed. "I'll get the money we can spare, and trust that George will make what bargain he can."

He came back downstairs, neatened up as well as he could manage, and she pressed a few coins into his hand, saying, "Pay no more than you must, and if it comes too dear, we'll do without. If you can get as much as five yards of solid broadcloth, that should be enough to replace what your brother's ruined since the last time."

"Aye, Mother." He put the money away and turned to Lemuel. "Let us be off, then. No time to waste, right?" Lemuel shared a private smile with their mother and followed George out the door.

The bay had settled down to its normal choppy conditions, and though the air still smelled heavy and almost smoky, and the sullen clouds overhead had a fell cast about them, George could scarcely sit still. He attended to the oars with alacrity, and once the sail was set, he examined the approaching town avidly, reaching down over the side of the boat to splash the cold water of the bay onto his face and hands, cleaning away the worst of the dirt from his morning's work.

Lemuel could no longer contain himself, and said, "I

understand that you have more interesting quarry in town than the cloth merchant."

George frowned and sat frozen for a moment before answering, "And what if I have?"

Lemuel, still guiding the boat, raised his free hand in a gesture of mollification. "'Tis none of my business, I know, but Father tells me that you encountered a girl who caught your fancy on our last visit."

His brows lowered, George muttered, "I should never have told Father anything about her. I did not look to find myself a laughing-stock."

"Nay, brother, I am not laughing. I am but curious . . . and as always, concerned for your welfare."

George said nothing, but sat looking over the side of the boat at the water as it slipped past, a frown on his face. Finally, he spoke. "I know not what to think, Lemuel. I do not even know her name, nor where to find her, but it is true that this girl haunts me. I passed but a few minutes with her by the clock, but she has accompanied me ever since. I hope to learn today whether she is a specter sent to bewitch me, and best left to memory, or a human person whom I can come to know and like."

Lemuel smiled with a knowing expression. "I think you wiser than some may give you credit for, George. The same may be said of all women, in truth, and all have aspects of both in them." He paused for a moment, and then added reflectively, "Indeed, the same holds true for all people whose paths cross ours."

George looked away, and though his face still bore a look of irritation, he no longer felt the flash of anger at his father and brother that had turned his veins to ice at Lemuel's initial question.

He maintained his silence for the rest of the trip, and he fairly leapt out of the boat when they ground to a stop on the shore beneath the village. Over his shoulder, he said, "I must go to the cloth merchant first, before I attend to my other business in town. I will meet you back here before the supper hour."

Lemuel called out to his brother's retreating back, "I will see you here, and I wish you well in all of your business today."

Chapter 8

George wrapped up his negotiations with the cloth merchant in short order. There was no broadcloth to be had at any price, only linen, and that at three shillings per yard, more even than he was prepared to offer for the broadcloth, though that would have been merely a point of negotiation—he knew that the going price was dearer than that.

However, since the cloth his mother had asked for was not available, her money remained unspent, and he was free to devote the afternoon to trying to locate the girl from the alley. He stopped in at the village tavern to get a cider and to hear what people there thought of the strange darkness of the prior afternoon, and found himself treated to all sorts of theories. The more cider he consumed, the less patient he grew with the explanations he heard offered.

They ranged from the mundane—merely a strangely heavy thunderstorm—to the truly bizarre—some plot of the rebels to demoralize the British—to the divine—a warning from the Lord above to cease the division and strife between the Crown and Colonies.

None of these particularly satisfied George, and he finally said so, in bluntness partly fueled by the cider. "You're all mad enough for Bedlam. No thunderstorm ever gave the air a reek of brimstone and such a dull and inadequate idea that is to explain a whole day gone dark. Nor have the rebels shown themselves to be the masters of nature itself, being no more or less men than any other. I will not pretend to speak for God, but I do think that if he were trying to warn us, he might choose a less obscure means of doing so."

The proponents of each of the theories he had summarily dismissed each shouted rebuttals, and he gave them all a dismissive wave of his hand, turning to the tavernkeeper to get another cider, so well had the last gone down.

"Nay, son," the grizzled man behind the counter said, "I think you've had all you can hold." He motioned behind George with a tilt of his head, and George looked around just in time to find one of the men he'd called insane reaching for his collar. In short order, he was lifted bodily from the floor, and found himself flying through the air through the doorway of the tavern, his arms and legs milling fruitlessly to gain control of his trajectory.

He landed in a confused and befuddled heap in the road, his breath completely knocked out of him. As he gasped for air and sat up, he was equally horrified and glad to find himself staring into a friendly face—that of the girl from the alley, who jumped in recognition, and then gathered herself and said, "You appear in need of assistance, kind sir. May I return the favor you did me the other day?"

She reached down to offer him a hand, and he took it, standing woozily and unsteadily. She looked at him more closely and exclaimed, "You're bleeding! Come with me at once, so that I may examine your wounds and clean them."

He started after her unsteadily, aware enough of himself to take a deep breath and correct his gait, at least for a moment. However, it was quickly clear that between the cider and his ejection from the tavern, he was in no shape to walk anywhere just at the moment, and he stopped to lean against the front of a building, breathing heavily.

The girl turned to see what was the matter just as his world turned dark around the edges and he sank to the ground. The last thing he saw was her rushing back to catch him as he fell.

He awoke in a dark, quiet room, to find a cool cloth draped over his forehead and the girl kneeling beside him with a look of grave concern on her face. When she saw that he was conscious again, she smiled, shaking her head. "We must stop meeting at such moments, my friend. I am not made for fighting, and you are not made for drinking. Let us both resolve to stick with what best suits us, hmm?"

He groaned, not really feeling himself to be equal to any more witty a reply just yet. The inside of his mouth tasted like he'd fallen face first into the pigpen, and his head ached. With a start, he sat up, asking, "What is the hour? I am to meet my brother and return home by supper."

She frowned slightly and replied, "You have missed that time by some margin, but I assure you that we will find a way to get you back home. Now, lie back down, before you make yourself pass again out of this world."

He found it easier to do as she told him than to argue the point, and he lay there for a moment, collecting his thoughts. Eventually, he came back around to the first question he had meant to ask her, should he find her in town.

"May I know your name? I should like to stop thinking of you as the girl in the alley."

She looked startled for a moment, and then laughed enthusiastically, covering her mouth and silencing herself when she saw him wince at the noise.

"I do prefer that you not think of me as an alley girl, it is true. I assure you that it is not my habit to spend time in such places, and it was only ill fortune that led me to be there when you first met me." She smiled ruefully.

"I am Louise," she said, "Louise Johnson, daughter of Paul Johnson, late of New-Hampshire, and only recently arrived in these parts. You are, I take it, not from the village proper?"

"Nay," he said, after taking a moment to savor the sound of her name in his mind. "I live on the larger of the islands in the bay, and visit the village only as I need to." He remembered then the money with which his mother had entrusted him, and cursed under his breath to find it gone.

Louise noted his alarm and asked with concern, "What is it?"

"I have failed my mother and have lost the money she entrusted me with." He kneaded his forehead with his hand and blew his breath out through his teeth. "Oh, I shall be called such a blockhead by my brothers, to say nothing of what my father will have to say."

Louise smiled weakly at him and took his hand in hers, saying, "Perhaps it is for the best, then, that you will be late returning."

He shook his head, replying, "Nay, that will but compound my sins." He sat up again, this time more steadily. "I must be on my way, to try to find my brother."

She nodded and released his hand, though he found that he

missed her fingers in his. Just then, a knock sounded at the door, and she frowned, standing and saying to George, "I should hope that it is nobody who might misapprehend your presence here, nor make assumptions about your occupation with me."

The door opened before she reached it, and George gasped as Lemuel stepped inside, saying, "Miss Johnson, I may need your help in locating my"—he stopped short. As he saw George sitting there, the brothers and Louise all gaped at each other for a long moment, with expressions ranging from incredulity, to confusion, to dawning comprehension.

Louise regained the power of speech first, saying quietly, "It would appear that some fuller explanations are in order."

Chapter 9

George shook his head vigorously, trying to clear his mind. Lemuel pursed his mouth firmly, then shook his head and closed the door firmly behind him. He went to the window and ensured that the curtains were fully drawn, and then came to sit on the side of the bed where George had been installed during his unconsciousness.

George sat up to make room for Lemuel, and Louise found a spot to take a seat at the foot of the bed, saying, still in a quiet, serious voice, "Lemuel, I think we must tell him all."

Lemuel shook his head again, his mouth still tight, and said, "Let me think for a moment, if you would." He stared off into the distance then, clearly calculating and leaving George to ponder all sorts of wild possibilities, many of which left him burning with jealousy and betrayal.

For once, though, he kept his thoughts to himself, as he waited for the truth—or whatever portion thereof his brother decided that he could handle—to be revealed. Lemuel and Louise were now engaged in an urgent but silent exchange of gestures and facial expressions, with Louise clearly advocating for Lemuel to get on with it, and Lemuel arguing for more time to consider.

Finally, Louise could take it no more, and began, ignoring Lemuel's glare.

"My name, as I said before, is Louise, though my surname

is not Johnson. My father is indeed lately arrived from New-Hampshire, but he came here with the Patriot forces that attempted to remove the British from Fort George here."

She looked down at her hands for a moment, an expression of pain crossing over her face, before continuing. "I accompanied my father here in service to his company, helping to ensure that they were fed and clothed. I came in my mother's stead, as she is still at our farm in New-Hampshire, caring for my newborn brother and my younger sister."

She sighed. "In truth, the attack on the fort was going poorly in any event, as our general and the commander of the fleet that carried us here were unable to agree as to whose responsibility took primacy in deciding how we ought proceed. The general wanted to press the attack with all dispatch, but the commodore wished for more certainty of success."

Shrugging, she said, "Some of the men excused him for his caution, particularly since his Marines had paid dearly in blood on our arrival to these shores, while others spoke of his reluctance in the most disparaging of terms, accusing him of cowardice in private, while attending to the forms of honor in public."

Her mouth twisted and she said, "When the British fleet of reinforcements sailed up the bay, it was immediately clear that we could neither prevail nor sail for home. My father took me ashore and we fled into the woods, where we watched them harry our fleet upriver to its destruction and the dispersal of those of our forces that did not die here."

Her eyes again dropped to her hands. "I did not want to leave the rest of the company to capture or worse at the hands of the British, but Dad would not hear of exposing me to that danger if he could do anything at all to prevent it."

Louise drew a deep breath and made questioning eye contact with Lemuel, who gestured with resignation for her to go on. She said, "After the battle was over, and the fleet removed back to New-York, or Halifax, or whence ever it came, Dad and I made our way into town, with the intent of finding some means of undermining the British from within."

She stopped and looked to Lemuel again, and he sighed and picked up her tale. "I have been active for some time now in the Committee of Safety for this district, and when Louise's father appeared in the town, we made ourselves known to him, and ensured that he had every appearance of having lived here for years, so that the British would not suspect him of being a Continental soldier."

He gave the girl a somewhat warmer look now, adding, "Louise has been instrumental in helping us to gain access to intelligence about the conditions within the fort, disposition of its forces and armaments, and the like. She has charmed many of the enemy into all manner of indiscretions of information." He saw George look up at this, with a stricken expression, and added hastily, "Her means of charming them have been innocent, and so all the more clever."

George gave his brother a tiny grimace, while chiding himself severely for even thinking that it was any of his concern what sort of charms Louise might have used in the pursuit of her cause.

Lemuel, unnoticing of his brother's brief inner anguish, nodded, almost more to himself than to George or Louise, and said, "With the information she and others have assembled, we are nearly ready to guide a strike against the British garrison, and so rid this district of their unwelcome presence permanently."

George shook his head to clear his thoughts again, and held up his hand to indicate that he needed a moment to absorb what they had revealed to him. His own brother, a spy against the Crown? And the girl from the alley, whose presence had been constant in his mind for weeks, a rebel's daughter, and a spy herself? Was any of this real, or was it merely a vision brought on by too much cider and too little rest of late?

Until this moment, the war was largely a distant fact in George's mind—sure, there had been some warm action within sight of the island for a few days the prior year, but even that had the aspect of a show being acted out on a giant and distant stage. It was exciting, it was inconvenient, it was even upsetting to see the new fort being thrown up where once squirrels and porcupines had frolicked.

But it had not yet become personal, a matter of loyalties within his own heart, of safety that could cost him his own skin— and that of his brother, and of this fascinating and now utterly mysterious girl.

Where was the claim on his heart? Was it with a distant King and Parliament, whose dictates had made life difficult long before the outbreak of war? Was it with the Congress, safely holed up in Philadelphia, distant from any real hazard? Did any of these considerations outweigh the connection to his brother, or the hoped-for connection to Louise?

And what of his uncomfortable discovery that he did care what sort of methods the girl might have made use of? Could he suppress his unbidden desire to see to her safety and his unwholesome curiosity as to the lengths her father might permit her to go in the pursuit of his objectives? Of course, he realized with a start, both she and Lemuel were already bait for the hangman's noose, and if he threw his fate in with them, he might someday join them in dancing upon the gallows.

It was the thought of watching them go to their fate, rather than sharing in it, and indeed, doing his personal utmost to preserve them from that horrible fate, that finally settled his mind, more effectively than even a month of sleep might. He felt a cool sobriety come over him as his decision was made.

It seemed to him that he had been in silent consideration of these many imponderables for a long time, but it was in truth just a moment later that he lowered his hand, took a deep breath, and said, "If I may be of service in your efforts, I should like to do so. How can I help?"

Chapter 10

The trip back across the bay in the dark was silent, guided only by a moon that rose out of the water ahead of them, just past full and shaded blood-red as a final echo of yesterday's evil omens. George's thoughts oscillated between the thrill of danger that came with having joined in a conspiracy against the King himself, distant though he might be, and the anticipation of returning home to the more immediate and nearby terror of his father's reaction to his belated return—and the loss of the money his mother had entrusted him with.

Lemuel spoke up from the aft end of the boat. "Father must know nothing of this work, George. He does not approve of getting involved, and I fear that his disapproval would grow to forbidding you outright from having any part in this. We must invent some reason for you to visit town more regularly than you have been . . . he and Mother already think that you are desirous of more frequent visits on Louise's account, though, so—"

"What?" George had been listening with no more than half his attention until that point, but Lemuel's last comment had caused his head to snap up as he peered through the darkness at his brother.

He could see only a quick flash of Lemuel's teeth as he grinned and replied, "They approve of you pursuing an interest in a girl, of course, though they might be less enthusiastic if they knew her kinship with a rebel, and her involvement in their activities." Lemuel inhaled deeply, his tone satisfied and relaxed as he added, "I must admit that it is good to finally be at liberty to discuss this with you openly, rather than being forced to conceal my activities from you, and to keep my thoughts entirely to myself."

George chuckled in spite of himself, replying, "I know that it is an unnatural act for you to ever keep any thought entirely to yourself." His brother's answering laugh helped George feel less apprehension about the difficult conversation ahead. "Have you given any thought as to what I should tell Mother and Father about my tardiness, and the lost money?"

Lemuel paused thoughtfully, and then answered, "I fear that the truth, or most of it, will be the easiest for you to be consistent in answering to. I wish that there were some way to shield you from the consequences of your errors of judgment today, brother, but you were foolish, and a price must be paid."

George frowned deeply into the darkness. It had been years since his father had resorted to the strap for any of the brothers, but he had a feeling that this might be a sufficiently serious set of mistakes to justify such punishment. He shivered despite the relative warmth of the evening.

After they drew the boat up onto the shore, operating more by feel and experience than from any other evidence of their senses in the deep darkness of the night, Lemuel accompanied George up to the house, where the brothers could see through the kitchen window that a hoarded candle burned. George swallowed hard and held back, knowing that the interview to come was going to be a difficult one.

Lemuel, shaking his head and assuming a sardonic half-smile, pushed past him to open the door. Their parents sat at the table, and both looked up sharply at the sound of the hinges creaking. Their father's expression shifted from drawn and weary to an immediate frown, but their mother's eyes were rimmed in red and bright with tears, and watching the look of relief that came over her face was like the sun emerge from behind a terrible storm cloud.

She cried out, "Oh!" and leapt up from the table to embrace George. As he returned her hug, he could see their father's lips purse further and his brows lower.

"I presume that you boys have an excellent reason for having caused your mother and I such worry and grief," he finally said, his tone suggesting strongly that he actually presumed no such thing. "You have some tale to share with us, involving, perhaps, British soldiers, pirates on the high seas, or damsels in distress?"

Their mother released George and turned to their father. "Give them a chance to come and sit down before you begin with your accusations and anger, Shubael. You leap to the worst of possibilities, instead of permitting them to lay out the causes of their lateness."

Lemuel ran his hand through his hair and said, "Mother, I am sorry, but his anger may well be justified. My brother got himself involved in a dispute of some sort at the tavern, was tossed into the street, and spent the afternoon recovering himself in the home of a friend of mine."

George's face flushed and he closely examined the toe of his shoe for a long moment before steeling himself to look up and face his father's flashing eyes. "I am ashamed of myself, Father. I permitted myself to be drawn into a petty argument, made some intemperate comments, and was removed bodily from the premises."

Turning away from his father, who stood with his nostrils flared, but as yet incapable of speech, George put his hand on his mother's shoulder and added, "I have lost the money with which you entrusted me for the purchase of cloth as well, and would ask how I may earn your forgiveness." He felt his mother's shoulder stiffen before she moved, dislodging his hand, to face him, her eyes showing equal parts pain and despair.

Shubael's eyes narrowed, and he said with a low, dangerous note to his voice, "You will start by finding some way to make whole what you have cost this family, both in reputation and in coin. Perhaps your clever older brother will have some idea of how you might begin to redeem yourself, but I am at a loss for ideas beyond that."

George felt his face burn anew, and he replied quietly, "I shall endeavor to do so, Father."

Beside him, he saw his brother's eyes light up in sudden inspiration, an expression that Lemuel quickly masked before saying slowly, "I may actually have an idea for some means for George to do that, Father."

"I welcome your counsel, but I would hear the details before I say that I am glad to hear that."

"I know a tanner who has been looking for an apprentice. His assistant was impressed by a British naval commander last year, and he has been unable to hire help since. It is not pleasant work, but it is an honest trade, and one which would pay a sufficient wage to make up for whatever George lost today."

George considered what little he knew about the profession of tanning. He had a sense that the labor with the bell scraper was downright easy in comparison with much that a tanner had to do, and that Ned Yoder, the tanner of whom he presumed Lemuel spoke, was best approached from upwind. While he'd long known that it was likely that he'd be apprenticed out eventually—there was not enough farm to go around between four sons—he had not anticipated it happening so soon, and before the convulsions of war had ceased.

On the other hand, it would put him in town a good deal of the time, where he could actually be of some use to the rebellion, and might even have a chance to further explore the enigma that was Louise's past . . . and future.

It would also, as Lemuel said, give him both a means to replace the lost money and a trade with which to provide for himself. He decided that he could get used to smelling bad, so long as part of that aroma was the stink of money.

Shubael, for his part, seemed to be considering the possibilities as well, and began nodding slowly. His expression was hardly any less severe, but he said, "See to the details, Lemuel, and bring them to me when you have them settled." Turning to George, his tone became stern again as he added, "In the meantime, we have a cowpen that has yet to be cleaned this spring, and I believe that might be a very good place for you to begin doing penance for your misdeeds."

Chapter II

Lemuel stopped by the cowpen the next morning before going over to town to look into the arrangements for George's apprenticeship. He approached George, caught a whiff of him, and shifted to a position where the breeze placed him upwind of his brother. "Have you any particulars that I ought request of Mister Yoder on your behalf?"

George stuck his spade into the ground of the pen and leaned on it, thinking for a moment before he answered. "Nay, I trust that you will make a good bargain for me on all accounts." He looked around to be sure that neither their other brothers nor their parents were anywhere around and then leaned closer to Lemuel, adding quietly, "I want to thank you for inventing such a clever solution to all of the problems we were struggling with. 'Twas a neat piece of work."

"Don't thank me until I have delivered upon my inspiration, brother. I know not whether a suitable bargain may be struck, nor whether it will answer to all of our other needs."

George smiled briefly, then his brow furrowed slightly. "I meant to ask—I understand why Louise, er, Miss 'Johnson' came to be in league with your Committee of Safety, but what drove you to break with Father's example and embroil yourself in the affairs of the rebels?"

Lemuel frowned in response and said, slowly, "That is a

long story, and one for a different time, but suffice it to say that Miss 'Johnson' is far from the first woman to be harassed by a British soldier who thinks himself our betters only because we were born on American soil . . . and there are good reasons that my wife refuses to visit town so long as the British garrison remains."

George gasped, saying, "Those monsters attacked Beatrice? When did this happen?"

"Keep quiet, George, lest someone on the other side of the farm hear you. Aye, she was attacked, and unlike our friend Louise, she did not have the means or opportunity to deny her assailant what he sought."

He drew a deep breath, and his eyes took on a haunted look before he continued, "There is no worse feeling ever in this life than knowing that one dear to you has been violated in such fashion, and that you are powerless to see any justice done."

"Did you not make a complaint to the commander of the garrison? The British fancy themselves to be represent civilized behavior and gentlemanly conduct, and I would think that they would leap at the chance to demonstrate those principles to the King's subjects here."

"I made inquiries, yes, but the officers I spoke to were uninterested in interfering with what they called a private transaction between one of their men and my wife."

He spat. "I marked that man's face, so that when the opportunity arises, I can make a special point of educating him about private transactions." Lemuel shook his head bitterly, and for the first time in his life, George saw a capacity for savage retribution in his brother.

George said quietly, "I apologize for the memories my

question stirred, and I look forward to joining you in taking revenge for the wrongs done your family."

"Do not apologize for a question honestly posed, George. Revenge . . . yes, revenge will be a sweet balm for the hurts to my pride, but it will do little to cure my Beatrice of her experiences."

He gave George another haunted look, adding, "I know not even whether the child she carries is mine, or some British soldier's bastard." He shook his head and inhaled sharply through his nose, doing his best to conceal his unshed tears. "In any event, the child will be raised as a Williams, and will know aught of its unclear heritage."

George nodded and pulled the spade out of the ground, eager to close the suddenly uncomfortable discussion. "I will hope for the best of your negotiations on my behalf today, Lemuel. It would be good to escape this foul task as quickly as is practical."

Lemuel laughed, no less willing to drop the subject, and replied, "I misdoubt that Father will let you off so easily, but I will do what I can on your behalf." He stepped away carefully, shaking his head at the aroma surrounding his brother. "I will come and see you as soon as I have news to report."

A week later, it was all arranged, and though the trip across the bay with Lemuel was routine, George could feel his heart race every time he thought about the prospect of taking up his new trade. He thought, wryly, that he already smelled the part, but he hoped that his work would be less strenuous under Yoder than it had been with his father driving him to compensate for the worry and fear that George had caused his parents.

The tanner had been all too happy to have an apprentice, as demand for his leather was stronger than ever with the presence of the garrison. Lemuel was pleased, too, at the access to the interior of the fort that this trade might grant, and had already listed for George the additional intelligence that he would most like to have, should he find himself within its walls.

"We have good knowledge already of the disposition of the forces within, and what their strength is, their duty schedules, and the like. What is less clear is information about where their powder magazine is located, how much they have stockpiled, what the state and quantity of their shot may be, and the like."

"How am I to gather such details in the course of simply passing through the gates, presuming, of course, that I ever have the opportunity to do even that much?"

"That will be a clever bit of work indeed, my brother, but I have full faith that you can discover some means of succeeding at it—but without raising any hair of suspicion as to what you are about. The British are constantly on their guard against spies of any sort, whether casual gatherers of intelligence or outright traitors. They are, as you know, utterly unforgiving of any act of treachery, and will reach for the hangman's noose more quickly than for the parole-man's quill."

George shot his brother a skeptical look, wordlessly accusing him of hyperbole, but Lemuel remained adamant. "Take no heedless chances, George. You can endanger not only your own precious skin, but also those of our families, and even our Miss 'Johnson' and her father."

At the mention of Louise's *nom de guerre*, he gave George a sly look, saying, "She sends her greeting, by the by, and asked me to convey to you the message that she should like to introduce you to her father once you have gotten settled in town. She suggested that you be sure to bathe thoroughly ahead of any such meeting, though, lest the first impression be more pungent than necessary."

George felt his face grow warm, and he scowled at the mirth on his brother's face. "I confess that I am surprised that she wants me to meet her father, with the impression that I must have made with my antics the other day. I proved myself amply to be neither a diplomat nor any great shakes as a fighter."

He shook his head, looking off into the distance at the waves on the bay. "I sometimes suspect that shoveling dung and reeking of the tanning-house may be the highest station in life to which I may expect to rise."

"Now, George, have some faith in yourself—and the girl. If she says that she wishes for you to meet her father, you may be assured that she is either satisfied with your station in life, or believes firmly that she can assist you in reaching some more lofty class . . . or at least a less odiferous one." Lemuel was doing all he could to not break into outright laughter, and George's deepening blush only made matters worse.

George reached over the side of the boat to scoop up a handful of water, which he flung in Lemuel's general direction—to no particular effect—before retorting, "I would sooner believe that she wishes her father to meet the newest member of the cabal upon which their return home may eventually depend, than that she has set her cap upon me, either in my current state or one to which she imagines I may aspire."

Lemuel shrugged. "Women are both less subtle and less obvious than we poor men suspect, brother. I cannot warm your heart with any reassurance, but neither would I counsel you to remain insensate to the potential. Take up those oars, and mind that you don't splash me." He busied himself with the sail, and George, still scowling, prepared for the work of propelling the craft through the final portion of the trip.

By the time the boat scraped onto the beach, he had forgotten his irritation at his brother, and it was replaced with high tension at the immediate prospect of launching into the process of learning the trade which at he might expect to spend the rest of his days. The question of Louise's intentions—or lack thereof—would have to wait until another day.

Chapter 12

Lemuel had made it clear that Mister Yoder—Ned, as he insisted that George call him—was not acquainted with the conspiracy, and that no details of it should be revealed to him. "Not that he is untrustworthy, mind you, but he is uninterested, and any who are not committed may be swayed by the promise of a reward for informing on rebels."

Though he'd always heard tanners referred to as reeking, George had never had quite so keen an appreciation of the verity of the charge as he did today. He stirred an enormous copper kettle full of hemlock bark as it heated over a fire of dried, spent bark. This part of the job was the most pleasant smelling, but Ned soon took the paddle from him, indicating with a quick jerk of his chin that George was to fetch a skin from the pile at the other side of the shop.

This was the part of the work that George most disliked, as the partly-cured skin was still acidic from being soaked in vinegar, which would inevitably find any tiny cut or scrape on his hands, and cause intense burning whenever he handled one of the hides at this stage.

The earlier steps—soaking the fresh hide in water to soften it, scraping the inside surface to remove any remaining flesh or fat, soaking it again, in lime this time, to loosen the hair and outermost skin, and then scraping the outside endlessly to get rid of them—

all of these steps were foul-smelling, disgusting, unpleasant, and exhausting, but the vinegar soak remained George's least favorite.

Along the way to learning about each of these steps from his taciturn new master, George had found a new appreciation for the simple leather that made up his shoes, a material that he had always more or less taken for granted.

The hide he pulled from the stack burned his nose and eyes with its vinegary odor, but he was thankful that the acid did not find any open cuts on his hands or arms this time. He delivered it to Ned, who shook it out and fed it into the kettle, using the paddle to push it all the way under the liquid.

"One more," he said, again motioning with his chin at the pile of hides. George fetched a second one, his eyes now watering at the vinegar vapors that wafted up from the thing as he carried it, and as Ned pushed it into the kettle, he nodded in satisfaction, handing the paddle back to George.

"Stir until the fire is out." With that, the man returned to the other side of the shop, where he was stretching a finished hide across a frame, pulling it taut and smooth with lacing around its perimeter.

As George stirred, he became lost in thought, staring deep into the steaming dark tanning solution. Adjusting to the rhythms of life in town had been a greater challenge than the simple matter of learning how to complete the tasks that he was assigned in the tannery.

Ned was unmarried—a fact that did not escape George's notice—and so mornings consisted not of cheerful chatter around the kitchen table while his mother served up breakfast, but instead a cold crust and a mug of cider, with a slab of indifferent cheese if

Ned was feeling generous.

The work of the tannery was unending, and a steady supply of fresh hides—or sometimes, less than strictly fresh—was delivered by the farmers and trappers in the area. Ned was content enough to let George handle the physical labor of moving the incoming skins, but he took care of negotiating the terms on which he accepted them with those who brought them.

Some customers paid in coin or promissory note to simply have the hides they brought processed and returned as finished leather; others were content to sell their hides outright, leaving it to Ned to resell them when he had completed their transformation into usable material. Some negotiated more complex arrangements with Ned, though, where he would take the skins on consignment, and pay the providers when the finished leather from them was sold to some third-party customer.

All of these bargains Ned recorded in his thin, reedy handwriting, and though George was educated enough to read a book—well, at least one Book—he could scarcely make any sense of the annotations Ned scratched into his ledgers.

They were fortunate in one regard for the presence of the British garrison in town—there was plenty of coinage in circulation. George heard one trapper complaining to Ned that in a village up the coast a little ways, nearly all business was conducted with promissory notes. "And how I am to carry about five lambs fresh-weaned in place of a handful of coin, or wait for them to be birthed and weaned, for that matter?"

In addition to the heavy hauling and carrying of supplies around the shop, Ned made George responsible immediately for any errands that needed to be run around town. These tasks George did not mind so much as the heavier physical labor, carrying as they did the constant possibility of encountering Louise in town.

That potential had not been rewarded more than twice, though, and each time, he had been on urgent business of one sort of another at Ned's bidding, and so had been unable to spare more than a tip of his hat and a nervous smile each time. Louise, for her part, had returned his smiles and had tilted her head in greeting, but had not gone out of her way, either, to have a longer word with him, never mind making further efforts to effect a meeting with her rebel soldier father.

As he stirred the kettle, George wondered whether that meeting would ever occur, or whether he had committed himself to a lifetime of smelling so bad that he must live on the far edge of town, with no particular reward.

On the other hand, he had finally gotten some satisfaction for his curiosity for the events of the dark day that had set this chain of events into motion. Travelers from further inland had reported finding immense quantities of ash having rained down in the storm that had accompanied the arrival of the darkness, and the prevailing theory now was that there had been some conflagration of biblical proportions at some place further yet inland.

Of course, there were other explanations still in circulation. The newspapers up from Boston were full of arguments one way or another, but one broadside in particular that had found its way to town was influential among many. George had read a copy posted up at the mercantile, and while he did not agree with its conclusion that a divine warning was behind it—he still held that some natural explanation was likelier—he could not help but admire the hand that had penned the coarse verse.

> *Ye Sons of Light who saw the Night, triumphing at High noon,*
> *The nineteenth Day of th' Month of May, mark well the dismal Gloom.*
> *No Orb above, in Course could move thus to eclipse the Sun;*
> *Then understand, it was the hand, of the eternal One.*
> *Who drew the pale, and sable veil, which interpos'd the Light;*
> *and overhead a Curtain spread, converting Day to Night.*
> *For every Town all burning down, and Forrest in our Land*
> *Would not create a Gloom so great; 'twas GOD's immediate Hand.*

He had not revisited the tavern, wanting to avoid a repeat of his last experience there, but he had little doubt that this line of reasoning would be persuasive to many he had encountered on that fateful day.

Another posting, though, had drawn his attention more closely, as it made mention of a total eclipse of the sun, not in the springtime, but late in the coming fall:

> *A rare and difficult event to observe, a Total Eclipse of the Sun is forecast for October the 27th instant, tho it will be visible only in the Northern extremities of this Colony. A mere handful of hardy souls along our Maine coast and points Northward in Nova-Scotia will be afforded the experience of the full darkness of the Eclipse,*

which is explained by our Natural Philosophers to be a shadow cast over the land by the Moon on a narrow track over the Earth's face.

Though it clearly did not pertain to the strange day of darkness, George was intrigued at the description of this new phenomenon, and took note of the date, just a few months hence. He did not doubt, however, that it would be taken as another portent of evil tidings, or Heavenly judgment upon the people here.

He shook his head and grimaced, still working the paddle in the kettle, until Ned called out to him, "Fire's out, and there is someone at the door. See what they want."

George set the paddle aside and went to the shop door, where he was surprised to find Louise waiting for him. "Good day to you, Miss Johnson," he said, suddenly aware of the disarray of his hair, the filth that had accumulated on his clothing, and the overwhelming stench that he knew attended this place and his person.

She nodded solemnly, and replied with uncharacteristic quietness, "And to you, George." She paused for a moment, and seemed to gather some courage before continuing, "Have you been avoiding me for some reason?"

"What? No, not at all! I have been full occupied with my duties at the tannery, and"—he looked away, abashed—"I know that I am no prize as company in this new vocation."

She shook her head, a small smile playing across her mouth, before she replied, "Nay, you are no rose, but you never were, and I should like to introduce you to my father at your earliest convenience." She leaned closer, and he could smell the fresh air of the summer day without on her hair as she said in little more than a whisper, "He may have need of your place here soon, for a project he is working on."

She leaned back, leaving George's head awhirl, as Ned came in from the workshop, saying, "What do you need, miss?"

She smiled brightly at him and said, "I came for some fresh laces for my boots. I broke one yesterday, and it has been vexing me most severely since." She lifted the hem of her skirt, displaying the offending lace, and the boot top that sat loosely open above it.

Ned returned her smile briefly, a rare expression, and said, "I have those, aye. I'll get one from the shop."

"Two, if you don't mind," she said, favoring him with another smile. George wondered what he could do to earn such a smile from her, as she added, "I should prefer not to have to walk about again with a broken lace, so I want to keep a spare."

Ned nodded and said, "As you wish," before disappearing into the workshop.

As soon as he left, she leaned forward again, and George nearly missed what she said in his enjoyment of her renewed proximity. "Can you come tonight to meet him?"

His heart suddenly started racing, but he said, as steadily as he could, "I will make the necessary arrangements with Ned. Is there some particular hour at which you should like me to arrive?"

"If you could come out at the change of the watch at the fort—when they lower the flag for the night—we would be glad to host you for dinner. You remember where we live, I trust." She wrinkled up her nose slightly, and gave him a wide smile. "Only, pray do take time to wash beforehand. Dad's nose is not so forgiving as is mine, I suspect." She leaned closer yet and brushed her lips against his cheek, before returning to a proper upright stance before Ned returned.

He was still blushing in embarrassment and surprise when Ned came in and dismissed him to the shop. "Finish with that deerskin I was stretching." George nodded at him to indicate that he understood his command, and then gave Louise a small, private smile before he passed through the door to the workshop, unsure still whether his feet were connected to the ground.

Chapter 13

Ned had only grunted in acceptance when George had asked to go into town on a personal errand for the evening. He hurried down to the creek behind the tannery and bathed himself, wishing that he had some of his mother's soap for the occasion—it was his first bath of the year, and he wanted to present the best possible face to Louise's father—but lacking that, he made do as best he could with plenty of water.

As for his clothing, he didn't have much choice—his second-best shirt was stained with the tannic soaking solution, and his best shirt hadn't seen a laundry since his arrival in town—but he made do with what he had. When he emerged from the stream and dressed himself, he couldn't smell any remaining odor—but then, he hadn't noticed the smell of the tannery, either, unless he had been away on business.

He shook his head and laughed at himself for a moment, reflecting that Louise's father was doubtless less interested in George's aroma, and more interested in what intelligence or other support the rebel cause could gain from him. As he emerged from the woods around the creek, he was gratified to note that the flag at the fort was just being lowered, so at least he would not be late for the meeting.

George made his way down the road to the modest house where he'd awoken after his ill-advised adventure at the tavern. At the door, he saw that Louise stood waiting for him, and her face brightened with a welcoming smile as she saw him.

"Mister Williams, so good of you to join us," she said, standing aside and gesturing for him to enter. "Dad, this is Lemuel Williams' brother, of whom we have spoken."

As George entered and his eyes adjusted to the relative gloom within the house, he saw her father rise from his seat in greeting. "Good evening, my friend," he said, with a firm, low-pitched voice. "Any friend of America is welcome at my table." George noticed immediately that the man was dressed in somewhat finer fashion than was common in his experience, and had a presence that seemed to fill the room.

"I am honored to meet you, sir," he replied, bowing slightly. "Your daughter has told me much about you, though I am deeply curious to know more, and hopeful that I may be of service to you and your friends."

"You have already been, Mister Williams. Did you not know?"

George shot Louise a puzzled look, but got only another of her enigmatic little smiles in reply. "I must confess, sir, that I am not acquainted with what you speak of."

Louise's father smiled widely, and he gestured for George to sit down in the chair across the table from where he now resumed his seat. "My daughter likes her little games as always, I see." He turned to her and said, "Louise, would you be so kind as to bring us each a cup of cider?"

Turning back to George, he said, with a small twinkle in his eye, "I am given to understand that you like your cider, though you may appreciate the moderating influence of someone more experienced in its effects than you are?"

George felt his face flush with warmth, and he replied as steadily as he could manage, "I have indeed learned a difficult lesson regarding my limits and the wisdom of exceeding them. But please, I beg of you, explain how this relates to some service I have already done you. I am both intrigued and confused."

As Louise set the cups before them, her father smiled again, nodding. "Of course. Well, as it happens, when you raised your little ruckus in town some weeks past, my daughter was engaged in an entertaining little bit of espionage herself, and the disturbance you created provided her with the perfect opportunity to accomplish what she was after."

He beamed at his daughter, adding, "I would prefer, of course, that she remain in the safety of our home, but I have long since learned that if I did not provide her with some guidance and supervision, she would simply undertake some task which she perceived to be of usefulness to me." He sighed, still smiling fondly at Louise, who was looking ever so slightly smug in return. "So, it is best that I give her little jobs to do, so that at least when she is exposing herself to some danger, it is one that I know about, instead of being something that will catch me by surprise later."

He turned back to George, clapped his hands, and grinned again. "In any event, we are here to discuss your role in our efforts here, and not my daughter . . . or at least, not that she has told me outright." Again, his eyes twinkled with some secret knowledge, and Louise looked away, feigning innocence, though her slight blush made George suspect that he had been a topic of conversations ranging well past his role in the rebellious conspiracy.

He chose to ignore this subtext for the moment, though,

replying, "Aye, sir. I have been given to understand that you are most desirous of details to be gathered from within the British fortifications, but I am sorry to say that I have not yet had any opportunity to visit there and gain such intelligence."

The other man waved his hand dismissively, saying, "We will worry about that in its time. At the moment, I am concerned with an opportunity that I have lately learned of from my friends around Boston, who tell me that we will soon be visited by an American ship, operating under the guise of a scientific expedition."

George blurted out, startled, "The eclipse? It will be seen here, then?"

Louise's father nodded, his characteristic wide smile reappearing. "I see that you are well-informed, Mister Williams. Most commendable. Yes, the eclipse will take place as forecast in this place, a few short months from now, and though the details are yet to be settled, we will be asking for safe passage for a small crew of men and their instruments."

With a gesture of both hands, he continued, "Now, this expedition will not be able to effect any sort of an attack itself, as such would be not only a violation of whatever safe conduct has been arranged for it, but as our experience of last year so clearly demonstrated, it will require a substantial force to retake this place from the British—and they are now even more established than they were when we last attempted it."

George nodded in understanding, and the other man continued, "We will, however, be able to communicate what intelligence we could gather with any agents whom we may be able to place among the crew of the ship that will transport the expedition hence." His eyes narrowed for a moment, and he said, almost to himself more than to George, "And with up-to-date information in their hands, neither the Legislature, nor the Congress will be able to excuse themselves from acting to free us from the Crown for all time."

He returned his gaze from the intense consideration of that victorious possibility to George's puzzled face. "I can see that you are wondering what part you may play in this?"

"Aye, sir." George looked over at Louise, who gave a tiny shrug, indicating that she did not yet know, either.

"Colonel Campbell is certain to think that there may be some conspiracy against his garrison among those of us here in the town." He held his hands up and raised his eyebrows, interjecting, "I have no idea what might have planted that suspicion in his mind."

He waited for George to chuckle at his expression, and then continued, more seriously, "I think it likely that the good colonel will forbid the members of any expedition that comes to these shores from any intercourse with the people living here, as a simple precaution against the transmission of intelligence or armaments." He nodded in approval. "I would do so, at least, in his position."

He gestured out through the window at the light of the setting sun sparkling off the water of the bay, where the island on which George had been raised lay, verdant and seemingly impossibly far away. "I expect that the colonel will restrict the expedition to someplace offshore, but within easy sight of the fort, that he may readily monitor their activities. It is likely, then, that he will suggest your family's farm, as it is both well-situated to his needs, and likely to be adequate for the expedition's."

Seeing the dawning comprehension on George's face, he

concluded triumphantly, "It would, therefore, be a relatively easy matter for you to arrange to be present when this expedition arrives, where you may then communicate unhindered with our agent among the crew."

George thought for a long moment, his brows furrowed in concentration, before answering carefully, "It seems to me that there are a great many places in this plan that depend upon matters which are beyond our control."

He ticked them off on his fingers, leaning on the table. "We do not know for certain that an expedition will be mounted. We cannot be certain that it will be granted permission to visit these shores. We do not yet know whether any agent of the American forces can be placed among the crew of such an expedition. You may know the colonel's mind regarding how best to accommodate the expedition while still ensuring his garrison's safety, but he may also surprise us at some turn or another. And we do not know that my family will be called upon to host them, should they arrive as you have predicted."

He sat back in his chair and smiled, adding, "Of course, I am willing to take part in this plan without reservation, otherwise."

Louise hid a smile from her father while his frown turned to a reluctant smile in reply to George's. "You are correct on every point, of course, but how else are we to succeed unless we take every chance that presents itself?" He thrust his hand across the table at George, who accepted it with a grin of his own. "Welcome to the Committee of Safety!"

Louise interrupted, saying, "If you two are finished planning the downfall of the British garrison here, I believe that dinner is ready for the table."

First to the table, she brought a loaf of fresh bread, just out of the oven. He father broke off a piece from the end, tossing it between his fingers, and offered it to George, who accepted it with a smile, tossing it about himself until it cooled enough to take a bite. Louise laughed at their antics, and accepted the next piece from her father, setting it on her plate in a vain attempt to set a better example for her dining companions.

While the two men chortled back and forth at the wonderful flavor of the steaming bread, Louise returned to the stove, bringing out a well-dressed pudding, unmolded on the platter and swimming in a perfect gravy. It filled the air with the enticing aroma of exotic spices and rich meat, and George's mouth began watering.

While he loved a good pudding, he was more accustomed to versions that were little more than some suet and meal, tied tight and boiled until swollen. This pudding was studded with raisins, and he could see pieces of pork embedded in the meal as well. "Miss Johnson, you did not tell me that you set such a table," he exclaimed as she sat down, and she beamed back at him.

"You did not ask, Mister Williams, and I am glad to be able to share it with you and Dad this evening." Her father grinned again at some secret joke that seemed to pass between them, and George frowned slightly, wondering if they were making sport of him.

He turned to her father, asking, "Shall I call you Mister Johnson, or do you prefer some other name?"

"Nay, Johnson will serve until the war is concluded, and then I pray that we will have an opportunity to introduce ourselves by our true names." George nodded, unsurprised. If the knowledge of Mister "Johnson's" real name were not present in the village, it could not accidentally become known to the British, who might well have come into possession of a muster roll or other means of identifying members of the failed expedition of the prior year.

"Would you like the first serving of the pudding, Mister Williams?" Louise's father held out a serving spoon to George, who accepted it with a grateful smile.

"Thank you, sir. I find that my day of work has left me famished."

As George helped himself to a hearty plateful of the pudding, and spooned up some gravy to go over it, Louise's father said, "Yes, I heard from your brother that you had found good employment in town, and that your position here might prove useful. It is curious, then, isn't it, that you may find more opportunity to serve the cause of American independence back on your farm?"

George nodded, passing the serving spoon back to Mister Johnson, who handed it over to Louise to serve herself before he took his serving. She dimpled at him, and took a modest plateful before handing the spoon back to her father.

"I must confess, sir, that while I am grateful for the opportunity to not only be located here in town where I can hope to be of service, but will also learn a trade, I am relieved at the possibility that I may be able to return to the farm, and yet be of greater use to your cause."

Johnson laughed heartily as he spooned gravy over the large serving of pudding he'd served himself. "I can understand that easily enough. When I have had occasion to visit a tannery, I have been impressed at how glad I am that they are generally located well outside of town."

He laughed with the others, and then added, "Of course,

there is no need for you to give up that opportunity just yet—let us wait until we know that it may be useful for you to be on the farm instead, shall we? And now, this delicious dinner needs to be appreciated without any further delay!"

Louise smiled again, and they set to, with their conversation returning to less complex topics, including speculation about the cause of the dark day, and gossip about the officers at the garrison.

At the end of the evening, as George walked back to the tannery, he absently rubbed his ribs where Mister Johnson's farewell embrace had bruised them, but all he was really thinking about was the feeling on his cheek when Louise's lips had again brushed against it.

Chapter 14

"**N**ed?" George entered the small, run-down house that he and the tanner shared. "I'm back from town, and have the items you sent me for. What needs to be done next?" He placed the parcels he'd carried under an unrelenting sun on the kitchen table, to await Ned's later instruction on putting them where they belonged. The trip into town had been uneventful, if sweaty—he'd hoped to see Louise again and receive another of her heart-warming smiles, but to no avail. Perhaps she was busy with some task for her father, or perhaps she was just attending to her duties at home.

In any event, the summer had brought no new word yet of any plans for a scientific expedition, although every time George saw Mister Johnson, the older man assured him that it was inevitable. George had begun to form his own opinions of the man's ability to tell plan from accomplished fact, but he kept his counsel.

Louise's friendliness to him had continued, though he had been frankly too timid to see whether it extended to anything more than friendly greetings and the occasional quick kiss on the cheek. Those encounters were enough to sustain him for days, though, with thoughts of her dancing through his head at every slack moment.

He continued through the house and into the workshop, calling out again, "Ned?" His brow beetled as his master still did not answer. He hadn't mentioned any errands that might bring him away from the shop that afternoon.

Walking toward where the large pickling vat steamed, he stopped cold in his tracks for an instant, as he saw two legs protruding from within it, and he recognized Ned's worn shoes on the feet.

George dashed over and dragged Ned's torso out of the vat, despite a sick feeling in his gut that it was already far too late. The man's joints were utterly slack as George pulled his limp body over the side of the pan and laid him out on the ground, and he could see that the lime had burned his face and eyes terribly. Where his hands had touched the liquid, George could already feel them starting to burn, and he felt a pang of sorrow for the suffering that Ned must have undergone in his final moments.

Standing and stepping away from the body, he plunged his arms into an open barrel kept nearby for emergencies, and moved them about in the cool water, rinsing the caustic liquid off his skin. He looked back at the body on the floor, and began to shake.

Ned had cautioned him that the heat raised by adding quicklime to water could be dangerous, particularly on a warm day. Perhaps he had failed to heed his own advice and had been overcome, or perhaps he had simply been stricken with a fit of apoplexy or a heart attack. In any event, he had died at his work, alone, leaving none but his young apprentice to mourn him.

George began to feel the first waves of grief break over him, now that the first, necessary things had been done. He knew that there were more tasks that he needed to attend to immediately, but for the moment, he could not formulate in his mind what they might be. He pulled his hands from the water absently and wiped them off on his legs, noticing for the first time that the fabric of his shirt sleeves was also damaged by the pickling fluid.

He pulled the shirt off and tossed it aside, walking the long way around to avoid Ned, as he returned to the house to get his other shirt so that he could go back into town. The odd stillness of his mind as he completed these small acts was mirrored by the unnatural stillness of the shop without Ned's ceaseless activity and work and commands. Once George was dressed again, he went through the front door of the house mechanically, still feeling calm, though his mind kept returning to the sensation of handling Ned's slack, lifeless body.

Without any deliberate decision about where he ought to go, he found himself at the door of the Johnson house, and, after a moment of hesitation, knocked at the door. He was surprised to realize that his eyes were streaming with tears, which he only noticed when Louise answered the door and gaped in shock at him.

"Whatever is the matter, George?" Her expression swiftly transformed from surprise at seeing him to concern.

"Ned—something happened to him." George had trouble even speaking, but eventually, he blurted out, "He's dead!"

Louise's hands flew to her mouth, and she exclaimed, "Oh, no! How? Where is he? Oh, come inside, and let us ask Daddy what to do. He has just now returned from some secretive errand, and is within."

She stepped aside, and George followed her, stumbling over the threshold. She reached out and caught his elbow, giving him a small, tight smile of reassurance as she did so.

Mister Johnson sat at the kitchen table, reading a pamphlet, which he had started to conceal on his lap, but when he saw George, he relaxed with a nervous smile of greeting. The older man saw George's still-streaming eyes, though, and stood quickly, rushing to his side.

"What is it that has you looking so unstrung, my friend?"

George took a deep, steadying breath, and said with as much cool collection as he could muster, "My master Ned has died in some accident in the tannery."

Johnson looked alarmed, but took a moment before he replied somberly, "I am very sorry to hear that, George. 'Tis a hard blow for you, I am sure."

"Aye, 'tis," was all George could manage to utter before tears overtook him entirely. Louise gently put her arm around his shoulders and guided him to a chair, where he sat until his sobs had subsided again. She sat beside him, and her father resumed his seat across the table from him, regarding the younger man with concern in his eyes.

Through his tears, he said, punctuated by hiccups, "I do not know why I am so distraught. Ned was—he was no kin of mine, but he was—was a good man, and I learned a great deal from him. And he died—he died alone."

Johnson asked in a comforting tone, "Have you any idea what happened?"

"It looked as though he fell into the pickling vat"—George held out his hands to give some sense of the size of the vessel—"and drowned before he could escape it."

Johnson gave him a puzzled look. "How might he have come to fall into this vat, and have been unable to remove himself immediately?"

George shook his head miserably. "I know not, only that the lime does give off a powerful lot of heat when it is introduced into the water, and with it being so hot already, it is possible that he simply fainted, or that he suffered some sudden illness and fell stricken. Once in the pickling liquor, if he were still sensate, he would have endeavored instinctively to escape, given the pain that accompanies unguarded exposure to it—but it looked as though he had simply leaned over the side of the vat and dropped in without a struggle."

Johnson winced in sympathy, and reached across the table to pat George's hand in comfort. "I think that we can guess that he was insensate, then, when it happened, and take what comfort we can from that."

He grimaced then, saying. "I should think that you will have to go to the fort and tell our self-appointed magistrates of this, that they may decide what is to be done with him—and with you."

"With me?" George looked up at Johnson, startled.

"Aye, your commitment to your master must be formally voided, and there may be other things that must be done, aside from burying the poor wretch." He sighed. "I cannot, of course, accompany you, as I do not wish to bring attention to my presence here, nor to our situation here."

George nodded, saying, "I understand entirely, and did not mean to ask for your assistance in attending to those details. In truth, I did not know where else to go, but now at least I have that much worked out."

He took a long, shuddering breath, and Louise reached around his shoulder and hugged him, resting her head beside his for a moment. "Go and do what must be done, George, and return here for supper, at least. I do not doubt that you would prefer not to eat under the roof where your master's corpse lies."

Despite himself, George shuddered, and she gave his shoulder a squeeze before standing. "It is best, I think, that it be done quickly."

George stood, too, and her father rose, offering his hand across the table. George accepted it, and the older man shook his hand warmly. "Come back when you have given them the information they need, and we can consider what we will need to do next for you."

"Thank you, sir," George said, and, wiping his eyes dry, he allowed Louise to lead him to the door.

"I'll see you soon, George," she said, and took him into her arms for a long, comfortable embrace. He tried to focus on her comforting presence, but his mind kept coming back to the feeling of lifting Ned's limp torso, which made it difficult to appreciate her lively warmth as much as he otherwise would have.

She released him and opened the door, waving to him as he walked away down the road, his eyes puffy and red, but his steps more sure now.

While he knew the way to the fort's entrance, he had never had occasion to go there before, and so he did not know what to expect. As he walked up the road to the gate, he could see a bored-looking pair of soldiers posted on guard at the entrance, apparently chatting with one another, their muskets held loosely in their hands. One of them spotted him approaching, said something to his companion, and both men sprang to a posture of alertness, bringing their guns up to their chests, pointing skyward—for the moment.

George held his hands before him to show that he was unarmed and no threat, and stopped where he was. One of the guards nodded and motioned with his free hand for George to approach, which he did with some trepidation, still holding his hands at waist level.

As he came within earshot, the one who had summoned him demanded, his accent harsh in George's ears, "Why are you here, and what is your business?"

George continued advancing slowly, answering, "I come to report a death by some accident at the tannery in town." The guard who had challenged him appeared to think for a moment, and then nodded to his companion.

"Wait here, Harry, and keep your weapon ready, in case this is some ruse." The guard turned and entered the gate, leaving the other man still posted at his station. George didn't think that the guard had meant to be heard, but just the same, his eye couldn't help but be drawn to the musket that the guard called Harry held across his shoulder.

It was similar in design to guns that George had used, its flint poised to strike the spark that would launch a ball through the air with deadly power, at the twitch of the guard's finger. What really drew George's attention, though, was the wicked-looking bayonet fixed above the barrel of the gun. Its polished length glinted in the sunlight, and the tip looked almost hungry to George's eyes.

Looking away from the gun with an effort, George tried to focus instead on the man who carried it. The man's heavy wool jacket—dyed in the notorious crimson of the British occupation forces—looked uncomfortably warm in the summer heat, and indeed, George could see a bead of sweat trickling down the side of the soldier's face.

The guard looked hardly older than George himself, and he was surprised to see that in spite of the face that the other man had his gun at the ready, and he was alone and unarmed, the soldier was frightened, his eyes darting about nervously when the colonist tried to meet them. George wondered at the fact that the garrison apparently seemed to this soldier to be so vulnerable that the unannounced presence of even a single colonist was cause for alarm.

Upon further consideration, it occurred to George that a guilty conscience could also be reason for the man's nervous demeanor. Had this man been involved in some violence against the Americans—had he, indeed, even been party to the abuse visited upon Lemuel's Beatrice? His heart hardened, and any sympathy he might have felt for the soldier's discomfort in the sun, or fear of attack by the Americans surrounding his garrison, evaporated.

George and the soldier stood looking at each other for several more minutes, neither one saying a word, and both frightened of, and angry at what the other represented. After an interminable span of time, the other soldier returned, saying crisply to George, "Follow me."

George complied, passing the soldier who remained on guard, but who now looked past him at the woods that closed in around the road up to the gate, scanning for any sign of a sneak attack. As George got downwind of the soldier named Harry, he could smell the sharp reek of fear that rose from him, and though he was keenly aware that his clothes were shabby and hard-worn in comparison with the other man's fine uniform, he felt some level of pride that he was, at least, not so frightened in every moment that it had permeated his clothing.

Within the walls of the fort, the overwhelming impression that George immediately got was of well-ordered activity, and a great deal of it. A squad of men were busily engaged in raising a new building—a barracks, from the look of it—along one wall of the fort, and another squad drilled in the clearing at the center of the walled-in space.

Small knots of soldiers worked at other tasks throughout the area, and at the corners of the fort, he could see guards in low towers, small cannon at the ready, with balls piled neatly, at the ready, should any ship or land force threaten this outpost of the Crown's authority over this part of America.

The guard led him to a squat barracks building to one side of the fortification, and brought him to one of the several doors that opened toward the drill field. He rapped smartly at the door frame, saying formally, "Lieutenant, here is the visitor of whom I informed you."

With a raspy voice, the man within the room replied, "Thank you, Private. You may return to your posting; I will send the orderly on duty to escort him out when we are finished here." To George, the man called out, "Come in, young man, and tell me what brings you to the King's fort today."

George entered the room, and saw a small man behind a large desk in the gloom within. The officer looked harassed and overheated, and did not evince an air of any concern at all for the mere death of a civilian nearby his garrison. George explained the events of the day to the man, and when he was done, the British officer scratched a brief note on a page and, as he wrote, addressed

George.

"I am ordering a detachment to investigate and determine whether there may have been any foul play; assuming that it was, as you say, merely an accident, you will see to the man's burial, and if, as you say, the man has no heirs, the detachment will take possession of any items of value that may be found in the man's estate in favor of the Crown, and will see to the payment of your indenture—but only on a pro rata basis. You will, of course, provide the indenture to the detachment as proof of the terms of that agreement."

He signed the paper with a flourish and shook a sand shaker over it, picking up the page and blowing on it to finish drying the ink. He called out, "Orderly, will you see this man out, and deliver these instructions to Corporal Featherstone?" Another red-jacketed soldier appeared from an adjoining room, saluted smartly, took the paper from the officer and motioned for George to follow him, and it was just that quickly that George's career as a tanner was over.

Chapter 15

Waking the next morning in unfamiliar surroundings, it took George a moment to remember the events of the prior day. After dinner, Mister Johnson had insisted that he stay the night, as there was no assurance that the detachment from the garrison would have finished their business yet, and there had been no opportunity to arrange for a burial, never mind any kind of services that were needed.

George was grateful for the invitation; although the necessity of sharing a bed with Mister Johnson was a bit uncomfortable, it was still less unsettling than sharing a house with Ned's corpse. He woke before his host, and while Johnson snored as enthusiastically as he seemed to do everything else, George thought about what he would need to do this day.

Although Ned had never spoken of his family, George wanted to find out if there was a family plot somewhere, or else make arrangements at the small graveyard at the edge of town. George knew nothing about what that might entail, and he worried that the British officer's offhand decision to seize the dead man's estate in the absence of heirs would make even that much more difficult.

George didn't know whether Ned's death was yet known in the village, but he was not looking forward to the sad duty of informing those with whom the man had done business over the years of his horrible fate. He also needed to puzzle out to whom he needed to speak about going about what arrangements were necessary.

He would ask Mister Johnson, but the man was too much of a newcomer in town to really be able to assist him in finding the right people to talk to, or making the necessary arrangements. By the time Johnson stopped snoring abruptly and sat up, rubbing his eyes, George had just concluded that he needed first to speak to the proprietor of the mercantile, who was probably the one person in town whom he knew well enough to ask for assistance with the tasks ahead of him.

Mister Johnson looked blearily over at George and said, "Woke up with a busy mind, I see." George nodded back at him somberly, and the older man said, "Well, no time like the present. Let us be at it, then."

The man leapt out of bed, and George followed suit, retrieving his trousers and pulling them on. At the other side of the bed, Mister Johnson was doing likewise, and he motioned for George to go ahead out to the kitchen, where they could already hear Louise working on stoking the fire.

As he entered the kitchen, she was busily tending something at the hearth, and faced away from the doorway. George sat at the table and marveled that the girl could already look so tidy, her hair up in a comb, and the laces on her dress neatly tightened and tied. He hazarded to say to her, "Good morning, Miss Johnson, and how are you today?"

She started, then relaxed, looking over her shoulder at him with a sympathetic smile. "I did not expect you so early awake, Mister Williams, after the shocks you suffered yesterday. How fare you this morning?"

George took a deep breath, and said soberly, "I am tolerably well, though I know I have another difficult day before me."

She nodded and turned back to the pot she was stirring at the hearth. "I can imagine," she said. "I am sure that Dad will be of assistance, as he can be."

"Indeed I shall," said her father as he entered the kitchen. "If there is anything within my power to do to assist you, Mister Williams, please ask without reservation."

George looked around at Johnson with a quick, grateful smile. "I do appreciate that, but the inquiries I believe I need to make today will likely require long familiarity with the affairs of the town, and I have already guessed that I will need to ask others for assistance of that sort."

Johnson grimaced briefly and said, "You are correct, though I do wish that my position were such that I could be more helpful to you."

"Do not worry on my account," George replied. "I will first consult with the storekeeper at the mercantile—he should be able to direct me to any person in town whose assistance I may need."

"A sound plan." Johnson nodded in approval. "Before you go anywhere, though, you must eat. Louise, what will you offer to break our fast?"

"Naught today but a thin porridge, Dad. We are in need of funds or other support to supply our larder soon."

Her father looked for a brief instant as though he'd bitten into something that had gone bad, then brightened and said, "I will see to that at my first opportunity. In the meantime, I do have a little money set aside, and I can give that to you after our meal, my dear. In the meantime, let us enjoy what we do have."

She smiled and dished out bowls of porridge, setting them before her father and George, then served herself and sat down. She waited until her father had said the blessing, and then they ate, each lost in their own thoughts.

George finished first and rose from the table. "I had better be on my way," he said, with an apologetic gesture of his hands. "I do not know how long my errands today will take, but I should like very much to ask for the kindness of your hospitality until I can find passage back to my family's home. I was pondering this morning, and I realized that with the British assuming Ned's estate, I must presume that I will no longer have room and board at his home."

Mister Johnson made a dismissive gesture with his hand, answering, "Of course, and think nothing of it. 'Tis the least we can do for a true friend and patriot."

Louise spoke up then, saying, "If you can wait but a bit, I should like to accompany you to the mercantile, since I have business there anyway."

George sat back down, smiling with genuine feeling for the first time since he'd found Ned. "I would like that very much, Miss Johnson, and I confess that I am glad for the excuse to sit and digest a bit before rushing out."

She smiled back, and asked, before taking another spoonful of porridge, "Have you any idea what you will do now?"

George shrugged, saying, "I presume I will go back to my former place at the farm, shoveling dung and milking cows." He sighed. "There is no glamour in it, but neither is there any shame."

Louise looked downcast as she continued eating. Finally,

she asked, "Is there no other apprenticeship you might pursue here in town?"

Her father answered before George could respond, saying, "When Mister Williams' brother and I made inquiries on his behalf, there were no other suitable openings." He shrugged, before continuing diffidently, "It cannot hurt to ask, of course, but if you will recall, it was actually to our advantage for him to be on the island this autumn anyway."

She frowned, swallowed the bite of porridge in her mouth, and said, "That might matter if we had any firm word of this expedition you are anticipating, but at present, unless you have not shared with me your counsel, it is still a speculation."

Her father's face turned stormy for a moment, and he seemed about to say something, but he visibly mastered himself, his nostrils still flaring with irritation at her defiant expression. After a moment, he said crisply, "Nay, I have not yet heard any new intelligence, but my intuition tells me that our nation will not miss this opportunity to make its mark upon the world of natural philosophy."

George, hoping to defuse what was evidently a running dispute between father and daughter, said mildly, "We can ask at the mercantile and about town, but if nothing presents itself, I am well-enough satisfied to resume my previous station in life." He gave Louise a small smile, adding, "I am sure that I can prevail upon my brother to bring me over to town regularly to enjoy your company, Miss Johnson."

She broke eye contact with her father, turning to George and tilting her head as she looked at him, her expression inscrutable. "Thank you for that, at least. I am finished with my porridge;

shall we go?"

On the road to the store, she was uncharacteristically quiet, apparently brooding over her argument with her father. Finally, she sighed deeply, saying, "I apologize that you had to witness that. Dad and I do not often row, but when we do, it is best that we spend time apart for a while, lest one of us say something that we will long regret."

George nodded thoughtfully, and replied, "I do understand, though my father is less likely to say something than to reach for the strap." He smiled ruefully. "I have learned to keep my counsel, rather than risk that."

They reached the front of the store, where two British soldiers were loitering. One of them spotted George and said, "You'll be George Williams, the tanner's apprentice?"

George, puzzled, replied, "Aye, until his death in an accident yesterday."

Louise gasped in shock as he first soldier took him by the arm firmly, and the other said coldly, "Ned Yoder's death was no accident; his skull was bashed in before he was dumped into that reeking vat. You are to come with us back to the fort, where you will be tried for the murder of your former master, and, if found guilty, hanged by the neck until you are dead."

Chapter 16

George sat miserably, looking through the front window at the red coat his motionless guard wore. The day was warming up, and sweat was already beginning to trickle down his forehead in the heat of the improvised cell in which he was imprisoned. The back window was closed up with stout shutters, permitting no cooling breeze to pass through.

The reek of the lobster stew that had been dropped carelessly on his table rose with the heat of the day. George wished that they had collected it after he had tasted it and pushed it away, disgusted at the unfamiliar texture, and dismayed at the roughly-chopped shell that remained around what meat there was.

Pushing the rejected meal out of his thoughts, he mentally replayed the events of the previous evening. After an initial gasp of disbelief, Louise had demanded of the soldier who had accused George, "What evidence do you have that the man was murdered, or that George might have done it?"

After a moment of surprise that a girl was upbraiding him so, the soldier answered, "It is your friend's misfortune that the company surgeon desired to examine the tanner's corpse in the pursuit of his studies of natural philosophy. As he did so, he could not help but notice that the man's skull was shattered—by a blow from behind, I heard him say."

He had taken a moment to glare at George, muttering, "The

poor devil never even had a chance to defend himself." Turning back to Louise, he had said, "As for cause to suspect your friend, it is no more than any frustrated apprentice my take it upon himself to do; the exact motivations will emerge once the lieutenant has had an opportunity to examine this monster."

Louise had pursed her lips, obviously biting back a retort, and had then gone to get advice from her Dad, and to see what could be done to aid in George's legal defense. The soldier who held his arm tightly sneered as Louise leaned close to George's ear and whispered, "I know you did not do this thing, my dear friend, and I will see you cleared of these charges, no matter what I must do." She had kissed him then, and no mere brush of her mouth against his cheek *en passant*, but a real kiss. He had to admit to himself that he did not truly know which had put his head the more awhirl—the kiss, or his sudden captivity and charge of committing a capital crime.

The worst part, he thought, as a fly entered busily through the breezeless window and flew about his cell seeking sustenance, was not knowing what was happening outside of the plain walls that held him captive. Had his brother been informed already? His father? His mother?

Despite his best efforts, he found himself sniffling back tears at the thought of his mother's reaction to the news that her son had been accused of killing a man. She would be disbelieving, and distraught, but would want to immediately fly to his defense, without reservation.

His father, he reflected, would want to hear the facts of the accusation first, and would listen carefully to the evidence presented of his son's culpability. Were there any witnesses? Was there any reason to suspect cause—had Ned and George not been able to come to a harmonious working arrangement, or had there been some quarrel between them? Was the act he was accused of within George's physical capacity, or did it require greater strength, reach, or dexterity than his son was possessed of? In the end, though, George knew that he would judge the facts presented and find for his son—and would not rest until he was exonerated.

Lemuel would be shocked, but all the angrier at the capricious nature of their occupying rulers. How could any foreign force, innocent of the relationships and dynamics of the community, presume to judge whether any there were capable of committing such a crime?

Hiram and Alexander would be snigger at George's predicament, but would settle in to his defense—if only to point out that their younger brother lacked the necessary determination and willpower to take a life.

George wondered, too, what Louise's father would think. Would he harbor any doubts about George's innocence, and mull over the young man's demeanor and behavior, probing his memory for any hint of falsity?

Most of all, he wondered about his fate, should he be unable to convince the self-appointed British authorities of his innocence. Would he truly never see another autumn, with the leaves turning a riotous exuberance of colors before they fell to the ground, to be hidden under a soft coat of new-fallen snow? Would he never know the joy of a day's salary well deserved, the company of his family around the table, or the sublime sensation of a second kiss from Louise?

George stood and began pacing around his cell, eliciting

a brief glance from the guard, who returned to carefully ignoring him, in favor of the normal daily activities within the fort. The key to proving his own innocence might well be to prove another's guilt, and so he began racking his brain for any hints of who might have committed such a heinous deed.

As far as he knew, Ned had been scrupulously honest, a firm but fair negotiator, and, if not liberal with credit, patient with those who owed him money or goods. He was not inclined to involve himself with the passions that divided the community, either over the politics of the war, or any other issue, for that matter. To do so would have required speaking more than five words at a space, and *that* was utterly against his nature.

George had not noticed any obvious theft, though, he was forced to admit to himself, he had not been looking for such in the wild and confused moments after he'd found Ned's body. He did not remember seeing any obvious weapon lying nearby, though the shop was well-equipped with various wooden and iron pry bars, paddles, and the like.

Someone determined to do Ned harm would have had little trouble finding the means to accomplish their foul deed close at hand. George found himself wondering, morbidly, how the killer had snuck up on Ned. He'd never noticed his master's hearing being particularly bad, and the floorboards of the shop were not always quiet. Whoever committed the deed had either been there with Ned's knowledge, or was exceedingly stealthy.

As the tannery stood in isolation at the edge of town, due to the frequently unpleasant smells attendant to the business conducted within, any sound of a struggle or argument would have gone unheard by casual passers-by.

George grimaced, and stopped to look out into the parade ground in the center of the fort. He noted that the barracks had seen visible progress since the prior day, and a different squad of soldiers—notably less precise—drilled under a frustrated-looking officer. A small group of soldiers was cautiously rolling a barrel out of a low, heavily dug-in building to one corner of the fort wall, and George realized with a start that this must be the armory that his brother had been curious about, on that day that seemed so many years in the past.

The other details that Lemuel had asked for were laid bare to his eyes as well, though he doubted that the intelligence would ever serve any purpose, nor indeed even reach the ears for which Lemuel had hoped to gather it. George sighed, and resumed his seat, waiting for whatever might come next.

He did not have long to wait, as the small officer he had met the prior day came to the door shortly thereafter, casually returning the salute offered by the guard, and saying to George with his raspy, mild voice, simply, "Come with me, Mister Williams. We have matters of grave importance to discuss."

George rose and followed the man, a feeling of dread taking root in his heart at the British officer's tone and demeanor. Back in the small room with the large desk, the officer waved George to a seat across the desk from his own, and sat down himself regarding George closely. He steepled his hands before his mouth for a long moment before placing them flat on the desktop and asking, in a pleasant, casual tone, "So, Mister Williams, what reason drove you to kill Mister Yoder?"

George resisted the desire to react with anger, and instead replied, as evenly as he could, "Sir, I did no such thing. The man was my mentor, and we were on good terms."

The British officer gave George an exasperated look, and said, "Please show me your hands."

George looked at him, puzzled, and the other man made an impatient motion with his fingers, summoning George's hands to the desk. George extended them, palms-up, over the desk, and more quickly than he would have believed the officer could move, he had seized George's wrists and rapped his knuckles against the desktop, so hard did he slam them to the surface.

George began to cry out in protest, but the small man shot him a dangerous look, silencing him instantly. He examined George's hands closely, then released one of them to reach under the desktop with one hand. In an instant, he whipped a small knife out with his free hand and drove it through the webbing stretched between George's palm and thumb, and into the wooden surface below.

George did not even try to master the urge to cry out now, shouting incoherently in pain and rage, and starting to leap up from his seat. The officer let go of the handle of his knife, now firmly stuck in place, and almost gently put his hand on the forearm of George's pinned-down hand, sliding it up his arm and pressing his elbow back to the table, which forced George back into his seat.

As George quieted and resumed his seat, tears streaming freely down his face as he stared in disbelief at the knife protruding from his hand, the officer asked again, in almost the exact same tone, "Why did you kill Mister Yoder?"

George repeated, with desperation in his voice, "Sir, I did not kill Mister Yoder!"

The officer sighed and scratched his scalp in thought, an

annoyed and impatient expression on his face. He reached out and pulled the knife out of the table—and out of George's hand—and began wiping it down meticulously with a cloth he extracted from within his jacket.

As George began to bring his hand back to assess how badly injured it was, the officer snapped, "Leave it there; I won't have you bleeding all over the place." Raising his voice, he called out, "Orderly! Bring bandages and rope."

The soldier delivered the items as commanded almost instantaneously, as though he had anticipated the order. Carefully not seeing anything that was happening in the room, he placed the rope on the table and started to hand the bandages to the officer, who dismissively waved for them to go directly to George instead.

"Wrap your hand and clean up your mess," he said to George, dismissing the orderly with another gesture of his hand. The soldier seemed only too glad to escape the room, but George had no attention to spare on wondering at that, as he gingerly prodded at the wound on his hand, wincing, and began bandaging it.

Standing, the officer snapped again, saying "Get that blood off the desk before it leaves a stain." George wiped his nose on his sleeve, and then bent to his task, blotting up the small pool of blood that had accumulated under his hand, and the droplets that had fallen from it as he worked on it. He didn't notice that his questioner had picked up the rope until he bent beside George's chair, lashing first one foot, and then the other to the legs.

It didn't even occur to George to resist or fight back as the small man tied off the rope securely and cut it at the knot. He moved behind the chair and threw a loop around George's torso, pinning his arms at his sides and effectively immobilizing him with another tight knot. George could hear him moving around behind him, but dared not crane his neck to see what the man was up to.

Without warning, another loop of rope dropped over his head and immediately cinched up about his neck with menacing tension. He felt the officer's foot on the back of his chair, and with the same conversational tone, George heard him ask, "Why did you kill your master, Mister Williams?"

Tears of rage and terror poured down George's cheeks as he replied in a near scream, "Sir, I killed nobody!" He heard the officer sigh in exasperation again before he felt the chair tip forward, with only the rope around his neck preventing his head from slamming into the edge of the desk.

He dangled there, the corner of the desktop mere inches from his eyes, and his vision going dark as he struggled to breathe, for what seemed an eternity before he heard someone come to the door and say, as though from a great distance, "Sir, there is someone at the gate who says that he is Ned Yoder's killer."

He heard his tormentor sigh as though he was set upon by all the petty frustrations of the world at once, before the rope around his neck went suddenly slack, his head met the edge of the desk, and he saw no more at all.

Chapter 17

George groaned and stirred, wakened by an intense, dull ache in his head, exacerbated by a fuss in a room nearby to where he had been laid down. His throat was raw and felt bruised, and his hand throbbed, but he was quite happy to find that he was on a thin, straw-filled mattress in a small, dark room filled with the reek of fresh sawdust, rather than being interviewed by Saint Peter at the gates of Heaven. His hand was still wrapped in the bandages he had been forced to apply for himself, but someone had wrapped his head to safeguard the swollen wound above his eyes.

"Although he is, of course, free to go, your brother is recovering from an accident that he suffered while under questioning," George heard the lieutenant's raspy, unctuous voice say. He couldn't hear the reply, but heard the officer say, "The man we are now holding for the murder of the tanner is demanding the privilege of being held as a prisoner of war, and claims that he is a Continental soldier, escaped from our forces last year when we repulsed their ridiculous little attack. He says that the man he killed was a legitimate target in an ongoing fight for this fortification, and that he is above civil authority entirely. Between you and I, I think he is quite mad, but he will dance no less gaily upon the gallows for it."

George could now hear Lemuel's voice more clearly, and

made out his brother's firm, but clearly shaken reply as he said, "I would see my brother now, that I may take him home to be physicked properly by his mother and family."

"But of course . . . he is just through there."

Even as George was still puzzling at what he had heard—the British officer couldn't have meant Louise's father, could he have?—his brother entered the room, worry etched deeply into his face. He rushed to George's side and fell to his knees beside the bed, saying in a low voice, "Oh, my brother, I am glad to see you."

"And I you, Lemuel." George was surprised at how his voice sounded, more of a croak than a regular speaking tone, and even these few words caused him a sharp enough pain that his hand flew to his throat. Lemuel took in his bandages and shook his head angrily, shooting a quick glare back at the door through which he'd come.

"We must leave at once, and you can tell me all that has passed once we are in a place where the walls do not listen quite so intently. I have much to relate to you as well." He grimaced, and stood, offering George a hand.

Standing was an exercise in finding new knots in his muscles and a multitude of scrapes and bruises, some of which he presumed must have been inflicted after he fell. Grimacing and breathing heavily, he leaned on his brother's offered arm and walked with him out of the room, and past the lieutenant, who smiled nastily as they walked by. George did not make eye contact with his tormentor, glad to be released from his ordeal.

This had brought him again to the question of who had come and confessed to the murder, but then he and Lemuel emerged into the evening sunlight, and the headache that burst past his temples was enough to completely take his mind off of the puzzle of his sudden salvation. He focused his attention on walking through the fort and out of the gates, where the same two guards stood post as had been there when he'd first entered—just yesterday?—to report Ned's demise. Neither of them so much as acknowledged the Americans exiting the garrison, one nearly carrying the other, and George could not help but feel a burst of hatred for their indifference.

As they got out of earshot of the guards, Lemuel said to George in a low, urgent tone, "I can see that you're in no shape to talk, so I'll tell you what I can, and we will discuss your 'accident' and other matters when you are more able."

George nodded tightly, seeking to avoid setting off a new explosion of pain within his head, and Lemuel continued, "I got word through our neighbor this morning that you'd been detained and were accused of killing Ned, so I came as quickly as I could." He shook his head bitterly. "Too late to save you from this, and too late to stop Mister Johnson from throwing his life away to save you."

George stopped dead in the road and stared at Lemuel, his eyes wide with shock. He croaked, "Is Louise all right?"

Lemuel's grim expression told George all he needed to know, and they set off again along the road, lit by long slanted shafts of sunlight that pierced the woods from behind them. "She brought her father the news of your capture, and she tells me that after a long argument with her, he confessed to her that he had gone to speak to Ned about releasing you on some pretext, to ensure that you were back on the farm for some far-fetched scheme he was hatching."

Lemuel's mouth twisted in another grimace and he said,

"Apparently, Ned refused outright to even consider it, and their argument came to blows . . . and at the end of it, Mister Johnson found that Ned had suffered a mortal injury at his hands. He did what he could to conceal his act, and slipped away, apparently not long before your return."

He shook his head in sadness and concluded, "After he told Louise all, he said that he would not see you hang for his crime, and resolved to demand his rights as a prisoner of war." With a wry smile, he added, "'Tis a clever gambit, trying to bind up the British in their own rules and codes, but that lieutenant does not seem to feel himself to be terribly constrained by such niceties. Mister Johnson may have misjudged, to his grievous loss. We can only hope that the colonel will impose some reason on him, and that Johnson will get to take his chances on a prison ship at New-York, instead of the much shorter odds of escaping a noose here."

George's hand went to his throat in sympathy, but he said nothing, hurrying alongside his brother. Lemuel said, "Now, we must return to Louise and apprise her of her father's captivity." He sighed. "I know not how I will break the news to her that she may soon be as good as an orphan here, with no means of returning to her family in New-Hampshire."

Shaking his head and grimacing, Lemuel pulled George along until they emerged from the woods at the edge of the village, long shadows preceding them along the roadway. "Can you now walk unassisted? It would be better to avoid drawing undue attention to ourselves as we go to visit the home of a man now known to be a Continental soldier. If we're not careful, we may yet find our way onto the lieutenant's scaffold."

George didn't point out that he was unable to be anything

but conspicuous, with his hat long gone in the struggles of the afternoon, and bloodstained bandages wrapped around his head and hand, but in any event, the roads along the place to the modest Johnson home was quiet. Lemuel strode up to the door and knocked, a quick tattoo that George guessed must have been some prearranged signal, for he heard the bolt being drawn without seeing any movement at the window.

Lemuel motioned for George to follow him inside, where they found Louise standing, her eyes red and puffy, but her head held high and proud. When she saw George, though, she gasped. "Whatever have they done to you, George?"

George held up a hand, wincing, and croaked, "May I have water?"

"Of course, and anything else you require!" She rushed off to fetch a cup and filled it from the pitcher on the sideboard. He drank gratefully, and then ventured another request, testing to see whether the drink was enough to ease the soreness in his throat. "Might I sit before I answer?"

"Yes, yes, naturally." She drew out a chair for him and sat in the one beside him, turning it to face him as she looked at the bandages, wincing in sympathy. Lemuel took a seat on the other side of the table, and George began.

"The lieutenant—I never did catch his name, only his rank—proposed to get the truth of how I killed Ned out of me, without regard for the methods by which he made me speak." He held up his hand and said, "He drove the point of a knife through my hand, then tried to strangle me with a rope. When he was interrupted by your father's arrival, he tired of toying with me and let me fall against his desk, where I broke my head."

Holding herself stiffly upright in spite of her obvious sympathy for his hurts, Louise asked, as evenly as she could, "And what of my father's arrival, then? Is he now subject to a trial by ordeal at the same hands as abused you so?"

Lemuel spoke up then, saying, "I do not believe that your father will be so tormented, Miss Johnson. Your father has made a bid for treatment as a legitimate prisoner of war, which, if granted, may spare him the gallows." He took a deep breath, and then said, "You must not dare to hope, however, Miss Johnson, as it seems more likely to me that the British will seek to simplify matters for themselves by punishing an admitted killer, rather than going to the trouble of granting him the privileges and immunities of a proper prisoner of war."

Louise kept her head high, though George could see that her eyes were welling up again with tears. She looked Lemuel in the eyes and asked, "When will he know his fate, then?"

He shook his head, confessing his ignorance of the answers she sought. It was only then that she began to weep, and George gathered her into his arms as best he could, rocking with her as she sobbed into his shoulder.

He felt completely drained, and could not think of anything better to do. Indeed, he felt certain that even if he had been fully possessed of his faculties, this would be the greatest service he could perform for his friend, just being there, as she had been for him just the prior afternoon.

His head was still whirling as he considered all that had happened in the past days, when there was a soft knock at the door, so soft that he scarcely heard it. Lemuel, too, cocked his head, as if wondering whether the sound were actually there, then rose to investigate, as George watched him and continued gently stroking Louise's quaking back. Peering around the shutter, Lemuel shook his head to George, and opened the door a crack.

He exclaimed softly and reached out, bringing in a large, cloth-wrapped crock, which he lifted, pushing the door closed again with his foot. He carried the crock over to the table, the noise of it scraping across the surface causing Louise to lift her head from George's shoulder to see what was happening.

Lemuel unwrapped the crock, and looked across the table with wonder as he opened it to find a rich, steaming broth within. Louise, though she had raised her head from George's shoulder, remained comfortably entwined in his arms. Their unknown benefactor had tucked a note inside the wrapping, which Lemuel held out to Louise. She shook her head, saying in a small voice, "You read it."

He opened it and read, "Keep up the fight. We are with you." He frowned and turned the paper over, saying, "That's all there is."

George could feel Louise take a deep, shuddering breath before she said, "Daddy always told me that the town was full of Patriots, and that they would rise when the moment arrived. He never expected to bring that moment about in this fashion, though, I wager."

Her eyes closed in pain, and when she opened them, she seemed to have found her old resolve and spark. She disentangled herself from George and leaned on the table, hands spread wide, her expression full of ferocity. "So, gentlemen, how will we go about effecting my father's escape from the British?"

Chapter 18

Before they could begin planning how to extract Louise's father from the hands of the British garrison, Lemuel argued for removing themselves from the house where the prisoner had lived. "If the British suspect that the Committee of Safety is considering such a thing, they may well have this house watched." He squinted narrowly for a moment, thinking, and then said, "You two stay here for a bit; I will go out and see what arrangements can be made."

He was gone before either George or Louise could object, and the two of them were left in the gathering darkness of the evening, with the hearth gone cold from inattention. Neither of them felt much like talking, so they sat quietly, side by side in their chairs, both of them simply glad for the other's presence.

Eventually, Louise said, "I should start the fire and light a candle," and rose from her chair, after taking George's unhurt hand in hers and giving it a squeeze. The returned pressure from his hand told her more clearly than words how much her care meant to him, how precious her friendship had become in the hours since the sun had risen that morning.

Aloud, though, all he said was, "Some light would be nice," his voice still gravelly and pained. She busied herself with the flint and charcloth, and soon enough, had a merry blaze going, though it cast long shadows about the kitchen until she lit a candle and brought that to the table. She also brought a spoon, which she offered to George, pushing the broth in front of him.

"Eat what you need; there is plenty here for the both of us." He nodded, and began to sup. For her part, Louise now looked around at the familiar kitchen, a wistful look of sadness in her eyes. George could tell that she was realizing that this house where she'd lived for most of a year now had become a home to her, and it pained her to realize that it was no longer.

Eventually, she spoke, her voice low and soft. "No matter what happens to Daddy, we will have to take our leave of this place," she said, and then looked George in the eye, adding, "I find that I am less eager for our return to New-Hampshire than I once was, and indeed, my thoughts of the future all seem to revolve around staying here."

She frowned slightly and continued, "While Daddy was in league with the Committee of Safety, and laying great plans for wresting this region back from the British, and all of those plans involved his continued presence here . . . I did not have to think about what came after."

She looked away, her gaze finding something in the far, dark corners of the room. "If Daddy can escape from his imprisonment, we will have to fly from this place, never to return so long as the British are present. If he is hanged like a common criminal, it will be my sad duty to take word back to my mother that she is a widow. If he is sent to languish on a prison ship some place, my obligation to him will be to follow him there to provide what relief I am able."

Her eyes returned to George's. "And yet, I want to find a reason to stay here, come what may for Daddy. Should he escape, we will likely be unable to travel in security for some time to come. If he"—she broke off for a second, choking down a sob—"if he dies, I can scarce travel alone. And if he is taken as a prisoner of war, I can as easily write him letters of encouragement and send him packages of sustenance from here as from New York City, or wherever he is sent."

She reached out again and took his hand. "I am torn between my duty to my father, and my duty to my heart, George." As she looked him steadily in the eyes, he felt his own heart beating wildly in his chest, and he didn't know what to say.

He held her gaze until he could trust himself to speak. He swallowed hard, willing his throat to work. "I cannot advise you in this, Louise, for my own heart clouds my reason. I would have you stay here always, but I cannot ask you to abandon your family, either."

She nodded, still holding his eyes, barely even blinking. After a long moment, she said, "I know that, and I just wanted you to know my mind, and the struggle in my heart, no matter what should come to pass next."

He replied, "Thank you for that," and then closed his eyes, feeling nothing but the soft warmth of her hand in his upon the table.

The door swung open then, startling them both as Lemuel slipped inside and closed it behind him. As though they had something to feel guilty about, they each quickly drew their hands back to their own laps before he could see anything.

"I have made the necessary arrangements," Lemuel said, without any prelude. "Louise, bring what you must if you were not going to be able to return here, but bring nothing that you do not absolutely need."

He turned to George, saying, "It is time for the Committee of Safety to see whether it may be transformed into a Committee of Action."

Chapter 19

"Tell us again what you observed of the guard towers." The grizzled farmer's tone was skeptical, but patient.

George repeated every detail he could remember about the postings he'd noted while he was within the fort, for what seemed like the tenth time. The members of the Committee of Safety sat forward on their chairs, gathered about a table covered in candles in a barn pressed into service as an impromptu meeting-house, questing for information about one aspect or another of the garrison —its readiness, its defenses, the personnel George had encountered, everything.

Another man, more sympathetic than most of the members of the Committee to the idea of mounting some sort of an attempt to rescue Louise's father, asked, "The squad you saw that seemed less experienced—do you have any sense of when they might be posted on duty?"

George shook his head. "I was not there long enough to observe any patterns in their duty schedule, but it did seem to me that most of the troops there were in good order, and well-disciplined."

Another man, around Lemuel's age, spat on the floor and remarked, "Not that Lieutenant Sauf, the one who interrogated you . . . his abuse of a prisoner should have netted him the severest of punishments, but we've heard before of his cruelty, and the colonel either turns a blind eye to it, or approves of his methods. In either case, he has failed entirely to impress upon his junior officers the need for civilized behavior at all times, particularly in dealing with those whom they would persuade to accept meekly their rule."

Lemuel blanched at the mention of Sauf's name, but said nothing. George did not have time to wonder at it, though, as Louise now spoke up. "Are you gentlemen going to debate like Congress, and give fine speeches until my father swings in the breeze, or are you going to take action to ensure his safety, just as he so many times risked his safety and gave up his home, his family, and his identity to fight to throw off the yoke of British oppression?"

A few of the men shifted uncomfortably as she glared around at them, her eyes flashing, as she practically dared them to argue the point with her.

The old farmer, whose role was not explicitly laid out, but who had served as at least a de facto chairman of the Committee, nodded, holding up a hand to calm the girl.

"Aye, we've heard all the information we may need to make a decision," he said. "The arguments for rescuing Mister Johnson stand at this: he has been a true friend of this Committee, at great personal sacrifice; he is energetic and creative in furthering our cause; and he is a legitimate prisoner of war under threat of prosecution as a common criminal, in violation of all standards of civilized conduct."

Louise sat back in her chair, crossing her arms and looking resolute. The chairman continued, "The arguments against mounting such an attempt are these: the fortification has previously proven impregnable, even to a full invasion force of trained and armed

Continental troops and marines, and even before its construction was complete; the garrison is alert for any such attempt, and is well-trained and equipped; and Mister Johnson, by even the most sympathetic accounts, did dispatch a respected member of this community without he was under any direct threat of violence from the same."

Louise began to protest, but he raised his hand again, this time emphatically, to silence her. "We will now take the vote as to whether or not to act. Those who believe we should attempt to free Mister Johnson will now show their hands." George, Lemuel, Louise, and the young man who had been accused of giving speeches all raised their hands to be counted.

The chairman nodded in acknowledgement, and then continued, "Those who believe that we should not attempt to free Mister Johnson will now show their hands." He raised his hand, as did the majority of the rest of the Committee.

Louise, her eyes already welling up with tears, stood and berated the men, her voice rising to a shriek. "You call yourselves friends of liberty, but when faced with tyranny under your very noses, you turn away, rather than risk your own skins in opposition to it. You gladly accept the sacrifices offered to you by men who travel far from the comforts of their own hearths, but cower at your own hearths when your sacrifice is suggested."

She whirled to glare daggers at one man after another, continuing, "You call yourselves men? I will go tonight and free my father, where you refuse even the attempt. We will fly from this place, and we will tell all who ask that the men of Bagaduce are both shy of battle, and unworthy of our defense or sympathy. As the pamphlet says, crouch and lick the hand that feeds you, and may history forget that you were our countrymen!"

She marched out of the barn then, her head held high and her eyes flashing in challenge to any who might try to stop her. The men around the table stared after her, some looking uncomfortable, others clearly just shocked at her words, and a few with outright anger showing on their faces.

Before any of them could speak, though, George stood, saying, "I am bound to help my friend, gentlemen, no matter how ill her words may strike you." He nodded as courteously as he could, and followed Louise through the barn door.

Outside, the air was still warm from the heat of the day, and he found her just out of the candlelight shining through the gap in the door, sobbing as quietly as she could manage. He said nothing, but simply gathered her into his arms, providing what comfort he could. She huddled into him, her shoulders quaking, and he quietly stroked her hair as he could feel her tears soaking through the cloth of his shirt.

He was still holding her when a young man dashed out of the shadows and into the barn, calling to the men within, "I have just heard from a soldier in the tavern that the colonel has decided to try Mister Johnson for murder in the morning, and says that he will hang the tanner's killer by noon!"

Louise gasped and went limp in George's arms, having fainted dead away.

Chapter 20

This was madness. Every fiber of George's being screamed that creeping through these woods in the moonless, dark night, with Louise's hand pulling him forward, was nothing more than a particularly elaborate means of committing suicide.

The wall of the fort loomed up at their left, and the only light they could see was a lantern at the top of the blockhouse ahead, marking the end of this wall of the fort. They had circumvented the guards at the narrow neck of land that connected the peninsula on which the fort stood by the relatively simple expedient of rowing across the bay to land far away from the road there, and had made their way as quietly as possible to the fort itself.

The light from the blockhouses at each corner of the roughly square fortification guided them to the middle section of one of the walls, and the plan was to scale the wall and sneak to the place where George had been imprisoned, on the assumption that Louise's father was likely now held in the same cell. Once they had located him they would find a way into the building from the back, or else distract or disable the guard, free her father, and return the same way they came. It was madness, but it was the only plan available to them.

After she had recovered from hearing the messenger come bearing his terrible news, George had taken Louise back to Lemuel's boat, with the intention of waiting for his brother to return from the meeting, so that they could formulate some new plan. The baggage carrying the pitiful few possessions Louise had gathered up in their haste to leave was already stowed in the boat, and George guessed that she would go back with them to the island, and perhaps stay with Lemuel and Beatrice for the time being.

Louise, however, had other ideas, and had soon come up with the wild plan they were now executing. She was her father's daughter, of that there could be no doubt, and it was out of sense of loyalty and care for her safety, rather than any conviction that her plan would succeed, that George had been persuaded to take part in it.

Now, as they reached the midpoint of the wall beyond which lay the low barracks where George had been held, it was time to try the chanciest part of the plan she had hatched. He gave her hand a small pull, and they stepped out of the woods surrounding the fort, and began down the side of the ditch that had been dug to protect the walls from a massed charge by an attacking force.

As a measure to break an infantry charge, it was no doubt perfect; there was no way to go through it quickly. However, for two young people who needed cover and quiet, rather than speed, in their approach to the wall, it was better suited to their needs than flat ground would have been.

They emerged from the far side of the ditch, coming to face the outer wall of the fort. With his hands more than with his eyes, George verified that what he recalled of the walls was correct—the outer surface consisted of roughly trimmed timbers, set into the earth and leaning slightly inward, presumably resting on a berm made up of the earth moved out of the ditch they had just come through.

He pulled Louise close to him and whispered, "The rope, now." He could hear her rustling slightly through the rucksack she had slung over her shoulder, and she quickly placed the coil of stout hempen line they had taken from Lemuel's boat into his hand. George found the end that he had tied into a loop with a slipknot— all the while trying not to think of it as a noose—and uncoiled the rest of the line to lie freely on the ground at his feet.

Taking a deep breath, he tossed it up the side of the wall, and winced as it bounced off and scraped down the side, seeming to him as though it was making more noise than a cow kicking over a pail. He and Louise both froze, their hearts pounding, for several long moments, listening for any reaction from the blockhouses or the other side of the wall.

Hearing none, George gingerly retrieved the loop end of the rope, his hands now shaking as his heart hammered in his chest. He ensured again that the rest of the rope lay free on the ground, and tossed the loop up the side of the wall a second time. This try, it stayed up, but when he tugged it to see if the loop would catch on a post at the top of the wall, it again fell slack and slid down the side of the wall.

After he had recovered himself and the rope a second time, he pulled Louise close enough to whisper again. "How many times will we chance some soldier hearing this and wondering whether an animal or a rebel lies without?"

She answered, in a grim, flat whisper, "Until we succeed or die trying." He knew that she could not see his answering grimace, but his resolve was bolstered by the quick kiss she planted on his cheek, and so he did not argue, instead preparing himself for a third try.

This time, he had gotten the range to the top of the wall right, and when he pulled the line, it held firm. He could feel the loop tighten as he drew it taut, until it was as solidly in place as if it had been tied there from within by an obliging British soldier.

He whispered again to Louise, "We need not die trying—at this point, in any case. The rope is secure."

She kissed him again, whispering back, "I knew you could secure it. Shall I be the first over the wall?"

"Nay," he replied. "If a British patrol awaits within, I would rather that I be the one to face them, while you escape to safety." This time, it was his turn to remain ignorant of her grimace. "Once I'm over, I'll tug the rope three times quickly to signal that it is safe for you to follow." He tapped her arm thrice to demonstrate what he meant.

She whispered in reply, "I will wait for your signal, but if you are taken, I will still come after you—it is the last thing they will expect." He shook his head at her stubbornness, but did not reply, simply pulling her close for a quick embrace, and then releasing her to begin scaling the side of the wall.

He was thankful for the slant of the outer wall, and for the roughly-hewn timbers, as they permitted him to pull himself up with his hands on the rope, and his feet finding toeholds. His hurt hand throbbed where he gripped the rope in it, but he gritted his teeth, refusing to acknowledge the pain. In some places, the logs of the walls had been sloppily trimmed, leaving limb stumps, and in others, notches from careless axe-work gave him relatively solid footing.

Before too long, he had reached the top of the wall, and

he slowly, cautiously, peeked over the unevenly-cut logs, straining in the darkness to see what was visible beyond. He could see the lights of the blockhouses clearly, and the window-openings of the barracks on the far side of the fort twinkled with candlelight.

Closer by, the building where he had been held was a darker form below him in the night, with pitch black darkness between the wall and the back side of the structure. No lights shone, though, in the shuttered windows that faced out at the wall, which made it easier to move about undetected in that space.

Looking down the wall toward the blockhouse, he could just make out that the far side of the palisade was a no more than a few feet from the top of the berm, and he pulled himself over with as much silence as he could manage, lowering his feet to the surface. Once he was steadily settled on the ground, he found the loop of the rope, checked with his hands to be sure that it was as secure as it had felt, and gave the three tugs of the signal he had arranged with Louise.

The rope jumped under his hand as she began up it, and he waited, cringing with every little sound her feet made on the wall, or faint grunt he heard from her as she struggled up the side. After what seemed like a lifetime, her hand met his on the rope, and he reached over with his good hand to find her other hand and assist her over the wall.

As she brought her legs over the wall, her skirt caught on the rough top of one of the logs, and she slipped the rest of the way over, falling to the ground with a tiny, stifled squeak. Again, they both froze, and George could swear that his heart was going to leap right out of his throat. Eventually, as they crouched together, his heart slowed, and he patted her softly on the back, whispering, "I think we are undetected. Are you hurt?"

She whispered back, shakily, "Nay, but I hope never to have to do something as foolhardy as this again." He grinned back at her, and sensed without seeing her answering smile. He stood up and pulled the rope up and over the wall, carrying it over to the inside of the berm, where he tossed it down the side.

"I think the inside is a gentle enough slope that we can just crawl down its face," he whispered. "I'll go first again, though, and you keep a hand on the rope, that I may again signal you when I am at the bottom."

"I'll see you there," she said, and he turned to start over the side. He found that the side of the berm was steeper than he recalled, and he had to rely on the rope to steady him all the way down. On no fewer than three separate occasions, his foot loosened some rock or pebble, causing it to fall down the side in what sounded like a minor landslide to his highly-alerted ears.

Evidently, however, no British soldiers were listening so intently as he was, and he soon enough had his feet on solid ground again, having now fully penetrated the fort's defenses. Again he signaled to Louise, and she made her way downward, with considerably less noise than he had. He still held the rope, until her foot passed his hand, and he nearly found himself being swallowed by her skirts, but he jumped back to let her descend.

As she came to stand beside him, he embraced her, his relief and nervousness leaving him nearly giggling aloud in spite of himself. She whispered, as she released him from her answering embrace, "What could possibly be so entertaining?"

"'Tis nothing," he whispered back. "Let us find your Dad now." He felt her nod in agreement, and he took her elbow in his hand to guide her to the end of the building where his makeshift cell had been.

It was a good thing that the room where he'd been held had never been built to be a gaol, for if it had, there would be no window, never mind one that could be entered undetected. Too, the relative newness of the fort, and remoteness of its position, meant that there was no glass for windows, and only shutters covered the openings.

Although his mind had been greatly occupied with other matters when he had been here last, he was quite sure that he remembered the room where he'd been held being at the very end of the building nearest to the gate, and that the shutters at the back of the room had been closed, apparently latched from without to prevent him from attempting to slip away.

Coming to the last window on the back of the building, he felt his way around the edges. He mastered the urge to shout aloud in victory as he found the expected latches, two of them. He turned them with excruciating slowness, trying to minimize the noise that they made. The first one turned more or less silently, but the second scraped across the surface of the shutter, no matter how slowly he moved.

As he finished unlatching the second shutter, he heard someone within stirring, and he froze, putting a hand out to Louise's shoulder as he did so. From inside the room, he heard a voice muttering a curse, followed by the single word, "Rats."

George felt Louise stiffen under his hand as she recognized her father's voice, and he had to restrain her from immediately flinging open the shutter to call to him. For his part, George was thrilled to have found the right place, overcoming all the odds that had been stacked up against them to get even this far. Now, they just needed a little more luck to extract him from the building and spirit him out of the fort to safety.

Louise shook George's hand off, and he realized that she must be trying to open the shutter when he heard the hinges creak slightly. She whispered into the gap, "Daddy?"

George could hear her father exclaim softly before he whispered back, "Louise?"

She replied, "Aye, here to rescue you, Dad."

He cursed again, under his breath. "'Tis a fool's errand, Louise."

"Nay, come to the window, and we'll leave this place."

"I cannot, Louise, as I am tied."

George went to Louise's side now, and opened the shutter the rest of the way. The darkness within the room reminded him of the time that Hiram had tricked him into sitting in an empty barrel, only to drop the lid onto it, closing him in. He whispered into the darkness, "I will come and release you, Mister Johnson."

"George? Who else is with you?"

"Just us."

Another whispered curse, followed by, "Very well." George hoisted himself up over the sill carefully, and stepped down into the room, wincing as the floorboards creaked slightly under his weight.

As he crouched beside the window, he asked, still whispering, "Are you guarded?"

"Nay, not that I know of. They are relying on my bindings to keep me from leaving."

"Well, let us see to those, then." George crept in the direction from which he'd heard Johnson's whisper, finding the man lashed to a chair, in much the same manner in which he'd been bound just the previous day. Working entirely by feel at the knots, he eventually had the other man freed. When he was finished, he found that his hands were shaking almost uncontrollably.

"Thank you kindly," Johnson whispered, and tried to stand. George heard him sit back down heavily and the man said, barely remembering in time to whisper, "Ah, give me a moment; my limbs are stiff from my confinement." George nodded, though he knew that Johnson could not see him.

In a few more moments, the other man stood again, then took a few shuffling steps. He whispered, "Which way is the window?"

Louise answered, sounding both relieved and scared, "Over here, Daddy." In moments, both men were through the window to freedom, and father and daughter were in each other's arms, embracing silently.

George was just about to tap her on the shoulder to remind her that they were still within the walls of a well-garrisoned enemy fort when a light suddenly shone through the gaps around the shutters of the next room over, nearly blinding him, and they heard Lieutenant Sauf's distinctive, raspy voice saying, "Thank you for the courtesy of your visit, colonel. To what do I owe the honor?"

Chapter 21

George crouched in silent fear beside Louise and her father, unwitting eavesdroppers outside what must have been Lieutenant Sauf's quarters.

Colonel Campbell said, his tone weary, "I think you know well enough, Patrick. I appreciate as well as anyone the need to maintain civil order, but we must do so with as gentle a hand as possible in these times, lest we stir up the local populace against us."

"Sir, I do not disagree, yet I think our experience in Boston and elsewhere has taught us that it will not do to let these colonials think that they may continue to exist in a state of nature, lawless and without any boundaries prescribing civilized behavior."

George's lips tightened in anger at the man's words, but the colonel answered, "Of course, Patrick. However, the best way to encourage civilized behavior is to demonstrate it. Here, let me share with you an example of what I mean."

George heard a rustle of paper, and then the colonel continued, "Here you see a copy of a letter, sent by the leader of the rebellion in Massachusetts Colony, this same John Hancock who was so very cheeky in affixing his signature to their 'Declaration of Independence,' as you will recall."

The colonel snorted, and continued, "Now he begs that we should give leave to a group from their local college who wish to come to this place to observe some astronomical event that allegedly can only be seen from this particular territory."

George could feel Louise's father stiffen beside him, but the man contained his reaction as the colonel went on, saying, "Now, I would be fully within my rights to deny his request, particularly given the vicious attack against this very garrison just last year." The colonel sighed and said, "But I will not do so, and in treating their science exploration with the gravity it would be due if it were, for example, from Oxford, rather than their little colonial school at Cambridge, I show them that we, at least, are a civilized people."

The speaker paused for a moment, and had apparently taken snuff, for he sneezed explosively and then blew his nose with great enthusiasm before continuing, "I should like to be considered by posterity as a friend of science, and what's more, the nature of their investigations here are such that it may enable all mariners to more exactly fix the actual location of these shores. Some calculation involving the exact time and circumstances of the thing they are to observe."

The lieutenant answered, "Sir, this is fascinating, but I fail to see how it pertains to my administration of justice here."

"I relate it by way of showing you an example by which you may profit, Patrick, and also because your interrogation may make this expedition that much more difficult to host in a civilized manner."

"How so? I but asked the boy a few pointed questions, and attempted to apply the necessary spur to his memory when he had difficulty recalling the correct answers."

"I have had a report of your methods, Patrick, and furthermore, there has been a formal complaint lodged against you by the boy's brother. What's more, our agent among their self-styled 'Committee of Safety' tells me that there is great agitation in the town as a result of the day's events, all of which will make it simply impossible for me to be as accommodating to these American natural philosophers as I might otherwise like to be."

"Well, sir, I shall be only too glad to answer to whatever inquiry you should deem necessary into the methods I used to question the boy. As for the crime of which he stood accused, as you know, we now have in custody the man who admits to having committed it, though he makes a novel argument that he ought to be treated as a prisoner of war, as he claims that this simple murder was, in point of fact, a legitimate act of warfare." The lieutenant snorted in derision, and Campbell appeared to agree.

"Well, we cannot tolerate that sort of thing, Patrick. I'll preside over the hearing, of course, as it is a capital case, and, again, we will observe all of the proper forms, as instructive to our colonial friends—and enemies."

"Yes, sir, and I shall ensure that you suffer no surprises in the conduct of your hearing . . . and that the murderer finds justice for his acts."

"I appreciate it, Lieutenant Sauf. I will let you get your rest now, as you have had a full day, and tomorrow promises to be no less strenuous."

"Thank you, Colonel. Your servant, sir."

The door to the lieutenant's quarters creaked open and then closed again, and the three rebels outside the building stayed frozen in a crouch as the British officer completed his bedtime preparations and snuffed out the light. By the time darkness and silence had returned to their hiding place, George's legs were on the verge of cramps in protest at their extended hold of their uncomfortable pose, and he was glad when Louise's father tapped them both on the shoulder, rising from his crouch.

They were thankful for the garrison's neatness—even the ground behind this building was clear of leaves and twigs that might have betrayed their movement past the lieutenant's window—and soon enough, they had found the dangling rope where George had left it, and were scaling the wall in the reverse of their entry into the fort. There was no way to retrieve Lemuel's rope, but George considered that to be an acceptable cost for the success of their project.

The woods were, if anything, even darker than they had been on the trip in, but they made their way through the trees as though their feet were guided by Providence, making little or no noise anywhere along the way. Emerging onto the beach, it took just a few minutes to locate the boat in the darkness.

Louise's father waited until they were at the side of boat before wordlessly embracing his daughter, then turning to give George a warm hug in turn. George returned the embrace with mixed feelings—the man had killed his master, and had left matters such that George initially took the blame for the crime. On the other hand, he had sacrificed himself once he had learned of George's predicament. It was . . . complicated.

As they pushed off the shore, George realized that he had given no thought to what to do if they succeeded in their absurd rescue, but after thinking for a moment, he began rowing back to the village to find Lemuel. The bay was quiet, as though even the water was in on the conspiracy of silence that evening, and they made good progress back toward the few lights still twinkling through the windows of the village.

The hard work of rowing had made George's head start throbbing again, and he thought that his hand might be bleeding anew, but oddly, he felt more alive, more joyful than he had in months. The path ahead might be deeply unclear, but it felt as though they had won a mighty battle against the British, and against the longest odds George could ever imagine facing. Snatching an admitted Continental soldier from the room right beside the lieutenant's, and better yet, from under the nose of the colonel, was a victory he could hardly have imagined in wildest flights of imagination.

How could a mere aching head and a little blood compare with all of that? This had been a day of triumph, and one that George would remember for the rest of his life.

Chapter 22

L ouise and her father were secreted away in Lemuel's house, and George was back on his thin pad, his brothers snoring enthusiastically away in the darkness nearby. Though it was closer to dawn than to dusk, with his head aching again, and his hand throbbing in synchrony to his heartbeat, he could not get to sleep.

Every time he closed his eyes, he saw Lieutenant Sauf's face looming before him, relishing his pain. He saw Louise, sitting huddled with her father at the far end of the boat, laying plans for their return home to New-Hampshire. He saw Lemuel, looking grey and haggard, and he saw his parents, their faces reflecting equal parts of shock and surprise to see him at their door in the middle of the night.

What he didn't see was a bright future. He no longer had a trade to look forward to, and would soon lose the cheerful prospect of passing time with Louise. Even his part in the local rebellion was clearly now at an end, as he had parted ways so definitively with the Committee of Safety over their decision regarding Louise's father.

For all that the day had ended in triumph, he remained shaken at having been taken for a common criminal, abused at the hands of a brutal inquisitor, and then forced by circumstance to drive himself to the very brink of physical collapse. And even still, he could not sleep.

He finally gave up, and made his way down to the kitchen, avoiding the creaky step halfway down almost by instinct. The warmth of the prior evening had given way to the dewy chill of a summer's early morning, and the banked coals in the hearth gave a welcome heat to the room.

He sat at the kitchen table and looked out the window at the first pale brightening of the rising sun, and wondered aimlessly at the spectacle, willing his mind to stop trying to make sense of the many bewildering events of the past couple of days. There was no sense to much of it, he knew, and any sort of new and rational direction for his life would be slow to reveal itself.

In the meantime, Pollianne needed milking every day, the fields needed tending, the pens needed cleaning, and he had a place in the world, even if it was not nearly as satisfying as the one he thought he might achieve.

He indulged himself for a few minutes with thoughts of what might have been, if only . . . if only Mister Johnson had come to him and asked him what Ned might think of releasing him from his apprenticeship. If only he had been faster that morning at his errands in the village, that he might have interrupted the argument that Mister Johnson had described, and prevented the violence that followed.

If only the wild plot surrounding this expedition from Boston had never been hatched, or he had found some way to dissuade Mister Johnson from thinking that it could ever amount to anything good. If only he and Louise could have continued, uninterrupted, their playful courtship—was it that?—and if only her father's escape from the British had not been so precipitous that they must now quit this place forever. If only he had never stopped into that tavern for a cider, or ordered the second . . . or ventured into the alley where his life had changed in an instant. Ah, if only . . .

He was still sitting at the table, thinking long, slow thoughts, when his mother came into the kitchen to get started on the routine of the morning. "No sleep for the weary, George?"

"Nay, Mother, nor for the wicked." He smiled weakly, and she returned the smile, a little unsure of his response.

Taking note of his wrapped hand, she said, "Have you refreshed your bandages yet this morning?"

"No, I have not, and indeed, I scarcely dare to do so." The wrappings were visibly soaked through with his blood, which had faded from the lurid scarlet of the day before to a dull, sullen brown. He knew that removing the bandages would be an exercise in pain, as even flexing the hand, he could feel that they were adhered to his wound.

He sighed and said, "Can you prepare some warm water to make it easier to dislodge them?"

"Surely, George, I'll get that started right away." She busied herself at the hearth, stoking a fire, and swinging the kettle over the flames once she had them crackling. Turning back to her son, she asked gently, "Can you tell me again how you came to be injured? I'm afraid that it wasn't very clear from what you said in the night."

He smiled grimly, and said, "It may not be any clearer this morning, as I am still further from a restful sleep, but I shall try to describe the events of the past two days more clearly." He outlined Ned's sad fate, and his own arrest and questioning, leaving out the details of the actual killer, outside of describing the man's confession at the gates of the fort, which had spared George further abuse and granted him his freedom.

His mother shook her head in amazement, saying, "How very much you have endured, my poor boy. If I had known that you would be exposed to such brutal hazards by taking up a trade in the village, I would have prevailed upon your father to have found some other means of enabling you to pay back your debt to him."

He began wordlessly unwrapping the bandage around his hand, and she continued sadly, "I knew that you would benefit from the opportunity to learn a trade, and though there are risks attendant to any apprenticeship, they do not ordinarily include being tortured as an accused murderer."

Seeing what he was doing, she bustled over to the table, gently pushed his fingers away from the bandage, and began unwinding it herself, pulling at the cloth stubbornly and deliberately, and removing it layer by layer from his hand. She came at length to a layer that would not yield to her gentle fingers, and fetched a cup of warm water to pour over it.

In spite of himself, George winced as the water soaked through to find the cut in his hand, but he managed to hold his hand still as she continued to work the bandage free of the blood, unwrapping it at last to expose his swollen and gruesome-looking palm. Turning his hand over, she looked in wonder at the wound on the other side, making a slight tut-tut noise with her tongue as she did so.

"Stay still," she said firmly to him, and went to rummage through the shelves at the other end of the kitchen until she came back with a small bag and a bundle of fresh bandage cloth. She dashed the water out of the cup into the hearth, where it hissed and steamed on the coals, and dipped up another sprinkling of hot water into the bottom of the cup. Opening the bag, she pinched out a small quantity of the herbs within, and dropped them into the cup, wetting them in the water with her fingertip.

"This will hurt, son, but you must hold still," she warned George, taking his fingers firmly in hers, and then overturning the cup onto his hand. The hot water and herbs dropped onto his skin and made contact with the wound, hurting almost more than the knife originally had. He managed to swallow the shout that he wanted to loose upon the sleeping house, instead gritting his teeth while his eyes trickled tears of agony.

His mother removed the cup and unrolled the new bandages, wrapping them over the herbs and around his hand to hold them in place as a poultice. "For as much as this hurts now, it will feel far better by tomorrow, and you'll scarce notice it in a fortnight." He nodded, tears still dripping from the corners of his eyes, not quite trusting himself to speak just yet.

She finished re-bandaging his hand and gave his fingers a little squeeze. "I wish I could just kiss this and make it all better, but you've found your way to injuries that exceed a mother's magic," she said, smiling.

He returned her smile weakly, and said, "I wish it were so easy, too." He looked away, shaking his head sadly. "Would that I had been there to save Ned from his attacker. I might have been able to talk him into some other course of action, and Ned might still be alive, but for my dawdling in town."

She took his chin in her hand firmly, forcing him to meet her eyes, suddenly resolute, and said, "Don't, George. You cannot hold yourself responsible for the wrong others do. Believe me, you will have enough on your conscience in due time, as a man who takes his responsibilities seriously; you need not take on the sins and errors of others as well."

After holding her gaze for a moment, he took a deep breath, saying, "All right, Mother. I'll leave the guilt to Ned's killer, and worry on my own affairs."

She nodded, giving him another small smile, and released his chin. "I know what you are doing, because I do the same thing myself, and I wish that someone had told me what I've told you, before I became too fixed in my habits."

A rumbling from upstairs signaled the wakening of his brothers, and his mother looked away then, her expression sad and distant for a moment. The moment passed, though, and she stood up, bustling over to the hearth, and saying to George, "I completely forgot to start the porridge, so focused was I on your hand."

Hiram and Alexander came down the stairs in a rush, and Hiram called over his shoulder, "I told you he was back." He stopped short when he caught sight of George's bandages, an oath escaping his lips and earning him a glare from his mother. "Did you wander in front of a moose or trip over a turtle or something?"

"Your brother has had an ordeal, boys, and I'll thank you to neither pester him about it nor tease him." George's brothers looked momentarily abashed, and sat down beside him, still gawping at his battered appearance.

Alexander asked, "Are you back to stay?"

"Aye, for the foreseeable future." Even as he said it, George had a pang of sadness at the remembrance of the departures he expected that future to hold.

Sensing that the prohibition on pestering did not appear to be violated by his brother's question, Hiram glanced briefly at their mother, and then asked, "What of your apprenticeship with the tanner?"

"Ned Yoder is dead."

"What?"

"How?"

"Were you hurt in the same incident?"

"When did"—

"Boys!" Both brothers turned simultaneously from George to their mother, who was standing by the hearth with a stern look on her face. "Go get your chores done, and leave your brother in peace."

They reluctantly rose from the table and went outside, where George could hear them excitedly speculating to one another as they passed by the window on their way to the fields.

"Thank you," said George, quietly.

His mother stood looking out the window at Hiram and Alexander as they walked down to the barn, her lips compressed in a firm line. "Neither one of them can do as they're told for more than a few seconds at a stretch. If I hadn't given birth to them myself, I'd wonder whose sons they were."

She shook her head again and turned back to the hearth to stir the porridge. She exclaimed to herself and may have even uttered a quiet oath of her own as she discovered that it was scorched, and then looked up sharply at George. "Don't mention it to your father; the flavor won't be much affected . . . and it wouldn't be the first time those boys had caused me to serve him scorched porridge."

He smiled and placed his finger to his lips, and she laughed.

"I don't mind it, Helen," Shubael said from the doorway

to their bedroom. She whirled around in surprise and grimaced, shaking her spoon at him in mock frustration. Despite the small smile that played across his mouth at the light moment, George could see a somber expression in his father's gaze as their eyes met.

Father and son nodded in greeting to one another, neither finding it necessary to say more. George's mother dished out the porridge, and his father sat across the table from him to eat. After he'd had a couple of bites, Shubael said, "I'll have you take up milking Pollianne again, if you don't mind."

George nodded, finished up the mouthful he was working on, and said, "I expected as much."

Shubael grimaced and said, "Your brother hasn't the knack for it, and the poor thing's nearly gone dry for his neglect, but you may be able to bring her back up to production." He pursed his mouth as though about to say something more, and instead gave a little shake of his head and bent to another spoonful of food.

George's mother looked over at him from the end of the table, where she was cutting carrots for a stew. She gave his father a pointed look, and he nodded, his expression inscrutable.

After chewing for a moment, he swallowed and said, "Thinking about having you help Lemuel. Beatrice is getting to be too close to her time to do much around their farm, and Lemuel's been needed in town a lot of late. Their place is suffering for it, and we've gotten accustomed to getting by with just the four of us here."

George bobbed his head, trying to keep the thrill that ran down his spine at the thought out of his voice. "I'd be glad for the opportunity to help them, Father. I owe Lemuel a debt of gratitude, and I am happy to be able to repay it." In his heart, he exulted at the thought of getting to be near Louise so much of the time. She and her father would have to stay out of sight until their escape from the area could be planned, but at least he'd be on the same farm with her.

"A man does what he has to do, until he can't. Worried that Lemuel's reaching the point of 'can't,' even if he doesn't realize it. With your help, he'll manage until Beatrice is up to doing her part again."

George nodded again, saying simply, "Thank you, Father."

"Day will come when you'll need the same, I expect, so give Lemuel as good as you'd hope to get. No napping in the fields." George's face warmed as he remembered the last time his father had caught him resting from his work.

"Aye, Father."

Shubael finished his breakfast and stood, leaving George at the table. Before he left to work on his morning chores, he said, "See that you get that bandage on your head changed, too."

"Aye, Father."

Did his father have some way of knowing that every fiber of George's being had yearned for a reason to pass more time at Lemuel's farm? Or was it truly as simple as he had presented it as being—a brother in need, and an unexpected solution presented by the catastrophes that had befallen George?

He ate the last few bites of porridge and stood, saying, "I should go over to Lemuel's house and give him the happy news."

His mother turned around from the hearth and said, "First, you will sit back down and let me have a look at your head, to make sure that your brains haven't started to leak out."

He sat, frowning, and said, "Yes, Mother."

Chapter 23

On the second day after George had been sent over to help on his brother's farm, he was carrying water in for the kitchen when Louise met him at the door, her eyes wide with fear. "It's Beatrice," she said, "It's her time, Lemuel is in town, and neither Dad nor I have any idea what to do."

George hurried to follow her into the house, and went into the bedroom, where Beatrice lay, covered with a blanket despite the warmth of the afternoon. She smiled nervously at him and pulled the blanket up to her chin. "My pains seem to have stopped, so it may be nothing, George. I'm sorry to worry you, but I do wish that my Lemuel was home."

George looked helplessly back at Louise, then turned back to Beatrice, and said, "Wait here, and I'll fetch Mother." Beatrice nodded at him, saying nothing, and George left her to her privacy. Returning to the kitchen, where Louise followed him, he said nervously, "While I am gone, start some water boiling; Mother may need it to steep herbs or something. I'll run as fast as I can, but if she starts again, just . . . hold her hand or something, let her know that she's not alone and help is on the way."

Louise nodded, still looking scared. "When Mama had her babies, I was too young to help, and Daddy had a midwife come to tend to her. I've never seen a baby born, and I am so scared that I will do something that makes things worse."

George gave her shoulder a reassuring squeeze, saying, "I've even less knowledge of the matter than you, but Mother will know what to do. I'll be right back with her." He released her shoulder and rushed out the door, breaking into a long, steady lope towards his father's home.

He arrived at the house to find his mother kneading bread at the table. George stood at the doorway, breathing too hard to speak for a moment, as his mother looked at him in alarm. Finally, he managed to say, panting, "It's Beatrice. She's having the baby."

"Oh! Oh, my. Let me gather a few things, and we'll go directly over to help."

George nodded, and stood holding the door frame for support. By the time she was tying on her kerchief, he had recovered enough to ask, "Are you aware of the . . . delicacy of the child's origins?"

She froze for an instant, and then nodded, her mouth a grim line. "Aye, and that's the last you'll say of it, young man. It matters not to your brother, and it matters not to Beatrice. No matter whether it has Lemuel's hair or only its mother's eyes, it is their child who will be born today, and that's all that matters."

He nodded in reply, and held the door open for her. She bustled past him, and together they made their way to his brother's home over the hill.

As they neared the house, they heard a blood-curdling cry from within, and although George started to dash to the door, his mother called out, "It is normal, George, and whether we arrive so out of breath that we cannot talk, or walk in ready to help, we cannot change Beatrice's pain in this moment."

He slowed and waited for her to catch up, saying to her,

"Why does she yell so loudly?"

She smiled serenely and answered, "All good things take some sacrifice and hard work, and it is hard to think of anything that is more of a good thing than a newborn baby, full of the potential of a life of promise. It is only fitting that something that wonderful should come at the cost of a large amount of hard work and sacrifice."

She shrugged, opening the door. "Today, there will be some blood and some pain. Tomorrow, there will be only my grandchild, and this will be forgotten."

Louise and her father sat at the table, both looking grim and frightened, and George's mother was taken aback for a moment to see them. "Lemuel didn't mention that he had guests staying with him."

Mister Johnson stood, saying, "I am James Smith, a business associate of Lemuel's, and my daughter and I were just here to keep company with poor Beatrice while he attended to some matters in town. We are, I am sorry to say, completely without any experience in the matter of childbirth, and so I am most grateful that you could come so quickly."

Louise caught George's eye with a questioning expression, and he replied with a tiny shrug. After considering the two of them for a moment, George's mother started to reply, but was interrupted by another wail from the bedroom. She nodded in acknowledgement of the introduction and then hurried out of the kitchen.

In the next few hours, there was little conversation, as the three of them listened to the laboring woman in the next room, and responded with alacrity to the commands George's mother came to the doorway to snap to them. Fresh water, a little broth, an extra blanket; Louise knew where everything she needed was to be found, and Helen was too concerned with helping her daughter-in-law to question their presence in the house any further.

Late in the afternoon, Lemuel returned home, coming through the door and frowning to see them all sitting at the kitchen table. George pointed to the bedroom, saying simply, "Mother is in with Beatrice, helping her bring your child into the world."

Lemuel said nothing to George, but rushed to the doorway, where he stopped and peered in, saying, "Is everything all right? Should I stay out here, or can I be of some assistance in with you?"

George smiled slightly at the determination in Beatrice's voice, as she said, "You'll not stray from my side, Lemuel, if you know what is good for you."

The sun was low in the sky by the time they heard a baby's thin wail, and, a moment later, George's mother calling out gleefully, "It's a girl!" After a few minutes, she emerged from the bedroom, looking tired by happy.

"A girl, and they've decided to name her Constance, Constance Williams." She sat wearily at the kitchen table, laying her head upon her crossed arms and smiling. "I am a grandmother."

Chapter 24

L ife had settled into a new and quite satisfying routine in the weeks since the upheavals in their lives, but George and Louise were still torn between enjoying each other's company in the present and agonizing over what the future would hold. They very deliberately did not discuss again what her choice must be—as far as George was concerned, she had made her decision clear at the disastrous Committee of Safety meeting. George's mother accepted the story that Mister "Smith's" daughter was staying with Lemuel to assist Beatrice, and without much further dissembling, her father's presence there was understood to be necessary to help Lemuel with some business matter.

Her father was still trying to surreptitiously get word out to agents in Boston or nearer by to see how they might be able to effect their removal from the district, and out of the reach of the outraged Lieutenant Sauf. In the days after Mister Johnson's escape, there had first been an ominous silence from the British garrison, followed by a quiet posting of a notice at the mercantile, offering a reward for his capture.

When that had netted no results, the lieutenant himself had begun leading armed patrols out into the town, using the pretense of checking the smuggling that the locals were always suspected of—and not without cause. Nearly every empty outbuilding and barn in the village had been searched at least once, and the patrols had actually found some smuggled goods, but they had, of course, found no trace of the Johnsons.

George had half-expected to be summoned back to the fort for questioning, as he had every reason to believe that the lieutenant knew something of his association with the Johnsons, but either the scolding he'd received at the hands of Colonel Campbell had made him wary of engaging with George further, or the gossip mill in town was far less efficient than George had thought.

In any event, the patrols did not venture out across the bay to the island, and George was left in an uneasy peace to take up his duties on his brother's farm. Events frequently seemed to conspire to throw him into proximity with Louise as he did so. She had taken over in the kitchen for Beatrice, who welcomed the relief from her chores there, and George was assigned to ensure that she had a regular supply of firewood, water, and other supplies.

Neither she nor her father could risk being seen outdoors, so while Mister Johnson avidly studied the latest pamphlets or news-papers that Lemuel brought back from town, or wrote another of his regular series of coded letters to be transmitted through various mysterious channels, Louise continued in her accustomed tasks in cooking and household maintenance.

It was easy enough for George to find an excuse to pass a late summer afternoon in the kitchen with her, so long as his chores in Lemuel's fields—and Pollianne's milking—were attended to. This afternoon, they were discussing the latest news of the war, none of which was particularly encouraging.

George said, "I was reading in the news-paper your father gave to me of the Iroquois war chief Brant—he has a fearsome reputation across the frontier in New-York—and yet I think it curious that his latest raids across the Mohawk Valley cost so few lives, in comparison with prior raids he and his friends among the Loyalist militia have conducted. He seems more interested in stealing cattle and burning homes than in collecting scalps."

Louise shuddered slightly at George's blunt mention of the most notorious tactic of the Indians, if lurid tales told by candlelight could be trusted. "Could not the Patriot forces in the area locate and destroy him, before he preys on more peaceful families?"

"Nay, by what I read, the chief has grown wise to the locations and dispositions of our forces across the territory that he ranges over. It is speculated that he must have access to some source of reliable intelligence, either from a turncoat among the Patriot militia forces, or perhaps through some false ally among those Indians who fight for us." George didn't often have the chance to introduce Louise to new information from her father's papers, and it gave him a sense of satisfaction to have that opportunity now.

Changing the subject, she asked, "Did you read the reports from the Southern Department?"

"Aye, and grim reading they are. Battles lost, many hundreds of American lives extinguished, and the main army on the run." George sighed. "I suppose that we here should resolve ourselves to suffer under the management of the British for all time. I have heard even that they have started calling this territory 'New Ireland.'"

He sounded sufficiently outraged at this idea that she gave him a little smile and asked playfully, "Have you something against the Irish, then? Did you not know that the Johnsons were Irish before they came to these shores?"

George remembered how he had hated the idea of the Irish

indentured servant whom he suspected his father might prefer to have in his place at the farm, and looked abashed. He replied, "Nay, I did not know that, and 'tis not the Irish that I object to, but the presumption on the part of the British that they have leave to apply whatever name they may choose to this territory, without offering its residents so much as the courtesy of asking our thoughts on the matter."

"Do boys ask the opinions of ants before crushing their mounds? The British see us as having little more import than insects, and our opinions are worth no more than that, either."

George looked alarmed at the analogy. "I should hope that they do not take it into their minds to scatter or destroy us wholly, as the child might do to an ant-hill."

"Nay, the Parliament is still sensible of the feelings of the people, and even if the King regards us as little more than insects to be removed by whatever force may be necessary, the people still retain some affection for us as a people. At least, that is what I have heard Daddy say, and I have no cause to believe otherwise, from what I see in the news-papers, particularly those Lemuel is able to get for him from London."

George frowned, saying, "I do not trust the reports from the London news-papers. They are written to sell copies on the streets, and not always to spread the light of truth."

Louise nodded, and rebutted, "Aye, but the letters submitted by subscribers do tell a story of a gentler sentiment than some in the service of the Crown may evince. They do not, of course, regard us as a co-equal nation, but neither do they wish to see our people removed from the earth over a mere political squabble."

She shook her head sadly, adding, "Not that there aren't

some who hold that view, but I must believe that if you walked down the street, or even visited the coffee-houses and taverns in London, you would have great difficulty in finding such."

"I hope that you are right in that belief, Louise, but the fact that we have some officers of the Crown in our midst whose every action seems to reflect just that view is troubling enough."

Louise gave him a sly smile, and said, "Lemuel brought back an interesting rumor about our Lieutenant Sauf yesterday, did you hear?"

"Nay, what has that creature done now?"

"He has been ordered transferred away on the next available ship."

"Is that so? For what posting?"

She grinned. "Someplace where there aren't any people for him to abuse, I should hope."

"What, has he committed some new outrage?"

"It seems that in the wake of Daddy's escape from his custody, Colonel Campbell conducted a thorough review of his subordinate's record for the first time in some years, and discovered sufficient irregularities that he could no longer justify keeping the man within his command."

She frowned, shaking her head. "The colonel had delegated to him responsibility for the discharge of civil justice, and it seems that the lieutenant was lax in those duties when a member of the garrison stood accused of some wrongdoing, but overly enthusiastic when it offered him the ability to mistreat the locals."

George rubbed his thumb across the scar on his palm and remarked, "Aye, I've some experience with that."

"Indeed. Lemuel said something that made me think that

he might have some experience with the other." George looked up sharply at her with a question in his eyes, and she continued, "He said that he'd sought justice for some infraction against Beatrice this winter past, and could get no satisfaction whatever from Sauf."

George's eyes went wide at this revelation, as he came to the realization that his torment at the lieutenant's hands had been nothing in comparison to his brother's. "Aye, he told me a little of that as well, but I did not know that it was Lieutenant Sauf who was at the heart of that miscarriage of justice."

A slow smile spread over George's face, too, and he added, "I should prefer to see him posted someplace where there is plenty of opportunity for him to face the wrath of those he has mistreated."

Louise returned his smile, saying, "I'd just like to find him alone in an alley some afternoon, and then he could face my wrath."

George began to chuckle as he pictured the lieutenant begging Louise not to kick him again, his self-superior sneer replaced with a look of outright terror at the apparition of pure vengeance in the person of this colonial girl. "Aye, I'd give a pretty penny to witness that, and I would not interrupt you, nor interfere in any way."

She began to laugh in response, and as the two collapsed into gales of laughter, George put his hand on her shoulder to steady himself. She drew him into a long, happy embrace, resting her head on his shoulder as they both continued to laugh, releasing months of pent-up emotion, fear, and longing in one shared paroxysm of joy. They had released each other, but were still wiping tears of mirth from their eyes when Lemuel came through the door, his eyes wild with excitement.

Without preamble, he said "The Americans are here!

They've just anchored in the bay, flying a flag of truce under their banner."

Mister Johnson strode into the kitchen and exclaimed, "I knew they would come! Oh, how I have prayed for this day, Louise—they may be our ride back home to New-Hampshire!"

Chapter 25

The American ship sat at anchor for a day, well up at the entrance to the bay, a longboat shuttling back and forth to the British garrison, carrying small knots of men who were barely visible across the expanse of the water. The next morning, as he attended to a fence damaged when a tree fell onto it in the night, George could see the sails of the ship fill up with the gentler breezes of the daytime, and it began to move up the bay.

He could not help but feel a shadow of dread at the sight of the ship, knowing that Mister Johnson hoped to depart forever within its hull, taking Louise with him. Yet he found that even that sadness was overtaken by his excitement at the appearance of a ship not under British command, and one that stood in the bay not to exert military control in one direction or the other, but instead to expand the body of human knowledge.

He was surprised to see that the Americans seemed to be sailing directly for the shores of his father's little cove, and as soon as he finished with the fence, he hurried to where Shubael was harvesting the last of the corn.

He called out across the field, "Father, it would appear that the Americans are bound for our own shore!"

Shubael looked up, unconcerned, from the basket, where he was arranging ears of corn, and glanced out at the ship, now only a few hundred yards off the shore, its sails already furled as it coasted in. George saw a splash at the back of the ship, and could even hear the shouts of the men who were lowering the anchor.

"Aye," he said. "The colonel sent a man over yesterday to inform me that he had offered the Americans the use of our farm for the pursuit of their scientific inquiries." He shrugged. "So long as they stay out from underfoot while we're getting the harvest in, I see no harm in it."

"No harm—" George broke off, hardly able to contain himself. "Father, this is the most exciting thing that has happened here this year!"

His father said nothing, but cocked his eyebrow, and looked pointedly at the scar that still stood out red and angry on the back of George's hand, matching the one on his palm. George made an exasperated sound and said, "The most exciting *good* thing."

"The pursuit of knowledge, it is said, is neither good nor evil, but only improves the human condition," his father said mildly. "I should rather have been consulted in the use of our property, but it is within the colonel's power to compel me to permit it, should I prove unwilling."

He shrugged again. "As there is only small inconvenience to it, I am not unwilling. They have been given instructions not to have any social interactions with us, and are to remain housed on their ship, so the colonel has not imposed hospitality upon me."

He waved in the direction of the barn, continuing, "That does remind me, though—they will require a dry, protected place for some of their instruments. After you have ensured that the pasture is secure, turn out the animals and begin cleaning the barn. I am given to understand that their equipment is of the highest quality available, and is very delicate. Clear out the manure, and then sweep carefully, lest some leftover bit of hay should become jammed in their gears or something."

George sighed as he turned to go down to the barn to get started. He turned back and said, "This means that we will see the eclipse here, then, I take it."

His father nodded in the direction of the ship and replied, "Aye, else there will be a whole ship full of disappointed natural philosophers out there. They have calculated the circumstances of this event quite carefully, and though the colonel has refused to grant them leave to proceed further up the river where they'd like to be, all agree that this location will let them complete their observations."

George nodded and walked back down to the barn. Although their arrival meant a fair amount of labor for him, he couldn't help but feel a thrill of excitement at the thought that his humble work would support a contribution to the expansion of human knowledge against the darkness of ignorance.

He was still sweeping out the corners of the barn when Lemuel came in, a broad smile on his face. "Well, brother, it seems that we will have closer contact with this expedition than ever we expected. Mister Johnson is so excited that it is difficult to even be in the house with him for long."

George smiled, though his eyes betrayed his sadness at the potential departure of Lemuel's house guests. His brother continued, though, heedless of George's reservations. "He has been practicing his introduction to the captain of the American ship all morning, strutting about the house and making grand statements about their shared patriotism and desire for freedom above all else."

He snorted and added, "At least I can escape the house.

Louise, of course, must remain out of sight along with her father, all the more so now that the colonel and his men will likely be in the neighborhood to keep a watch over the Americans, and Beatrice must stay with the baby."

George nodded, and reached up to sweep cobwebs from the rafters overhead. Although he did not think that they were likely to interfere with the expedition's instruments, they gave the barn an air of ill-maintenance, and he had determined to make everything as tidy as possible for their visitors.

"What of the eclipse itself, Lemuel? Will it be akin to the day of darkness that we experienced earlier this year? Indeed, might that have simply been another eclipse?"

"Nay, from what I have read, eclipses do not often come to the same place on earth, and never so quickly."

"Could the calculations have been off by a few months, and caused the expedition to miss their target entirely?"

"Considering that the expedition leader, a Doctor Williams—a strange coincidence, that he should share our surname!—has published his calculated predictions of the event to an accuracy of mere minutes, I misdoubt that they could have so badly missed their intended observations. No, that was something else entirely, and I expect that the coming eclipse will be quite different to experience."

George nodded, and continued sweeping cobwebs. "And when is this predicted event to take place?"

"It is to be just nine days hence, at the eleventh hour of the day, reaching its culmination just at noon, as the sun stands high overhead."

George stopped for a moment, holding the broom up as he

contemplated this information. "How curious it will be," he said, finally, "that when we ought to be in the brightest part of the day, we shall instead be plunged into total darkness." He shuddered, and continued cleaning.

"It will be an experience that will mark you for the rest of your days, brother," said Lemuel. "So am I led to expect, and so I do believe." He looked up at the sun now, and said, "I shall go now and see whether any from the ship are of a mind to further educate me on these matters."

He was back shortly, frowning. "Though they wave back when I wave to them, none has come ashore here. The British have sent a barge up the river, bearing some men from the ship, but none have seen fit to come and visit with their hosts? It is exceedingly strange." His expression reflected his frustration.

George said nothing, being engaged in sweeping out one of the stalls that was in active use. Unlike the dryer corners of the barn, this one was highly aromatic, and it was all that George could do to keep from adding to the mess himself, never mind holding a conversation.

He emerged from the stall, gasping for fresh air, and said crossly, "Do you think you could help me out a bit, by fetching me a couple of buckets of seawater to dash across this floor and clean it?"

"Certainly, but I think I may only be able to assist you with one load, as Beatrice expected me back before sundown." He rummaged through the corner where various tools were stacked and pulled out the water yoke Shubael had fashioned, placed its worn, smooth surface across his shoulders, and then bent to hook the handles of the buckets, one on each side.

George continued sweeping spilled grain and hay out of the back door of the barn, and though he permitted himself a flash of irritation at his brother for his ever-convenient timing, he reminded himself of all that Lemuel had done for him in the past several months, which helped him to prevent the spark of irritation from finding ready tinder and setting off a firestorm of resentment.

By the time Lemuel returned, buckets full to the top with clean, fresh seawater, George was glad to see him, and made good use of the water, cleaning three of the five stalls to his satisfaction. Lemuel nodded at the remaining stalls and said, "I'll get another load of water, and then it looks as though your work here is done."

"Aye, and thank you, Lemuel."

"You are welcome, George." George watched his brother walk down the hill to the bay, the American ship standing at anchor just offshore in the cove. He could already picture the ship weighing anchor and shaking out its sails to go back home, with a precious cargo including Louise's heart—and his. In a span of mere days, perhaps fewer than he had fingers, she would disappear from his life forever, and there was nothing he could do to change that.

He savagely wiped away the tear that trickled down his cheek and went back inside to sweep the barn again.

Chapter 26

The preparations that the members of the expedition undertook for their observations were both painstaking and mysterious to George. Within the barn, which Doctor Williams declared to be perfectly satisfactory—"Nearly as clean as any classroom in which I have studied or taught!"—there now stood a marvelous mechanical clock, with hands that not only counted off the hours, but also the minutes and even the seconds.

The inner workings of the machine seemed to be made mostly of thousands of tiny brass gears and cogs, but George only got a glance of them as the students in the expedition assembled the case around the clock, taking it out of its sturdy crate carried ashore overhead through the surf, with cautious hands lined up along both sides of the box.

One of the students pointed out the pendulum that swung ponderously back and forth under the main workings of the clock and explained, "That's made of two different metals, arrayed such that it will adjust itself for complete accuracy, even when the temperature changes. It's an amazing advance in the precision of timekeeping, and we're very fortunate to have this one."

George didn't need to be told that he should not even so much as breathe hard in the vicinity of this intricate mechanism. For that matter, none of the instruments the work party reverently brought up to the barn invited close examination by an untrained hand.

Four telescopes, fitted with all sorts of devices for taking detailed measurements, a device that the students showed George could be used to find an exact measurement of level, and then used to survey the terrain surrounding their location, a thing that seemed to be all brass arms and hinges that they called an octant—"The doctor will use it to measure the height of the sun above the horizon, which he can then use to determine our latitude, given the time"—and no less than three large compasses, all of which seemed to George to point in the same general direction of Lemuel's house.

After the instruments were unpacked and set up, Doctor Williams hurriedly took a series of measurements with one of the telescopes, and retreated to a small table, where he sat and frenetically scribbled out figures for a long while.

The next day, a thick fog obscured the sky at daybreak, persisting all through the afternoon. It utterly frustrated any attempt to take a reliable observation of the sky, but the students along on the expedition took advantage of the lull in philosophical work to pursue some more prosaic labor. They busied themselves with arranging sleeping quarters in the stalls—which made George exceptionally glad that he had taken such care to clean them—and even set up a canvas tent in the open space in the center of the barn. Lemuel arrived during this process and helped to drive the stakes into the floor that it would stand stable.

As they worked, the student setting up the tent explained their actions of the previous days. "We were told that we were to have no direct contact with the people living on these shores, as the British commander of these parts fears that we might be part of some conspiracy to overthrow his position here."

Lemuel leaned close and said quietly, "I know you are not a

part of any such conspiracy, but there is a small matter with which we here could use your assistance."

The student looked at him with a raised eyebrow, and said, "We cannot endanger our scientific mission here by becoming involved in any military intrigues. Understand that we are, of course, sensible of your position under the occupation of the Crown's forces, but we undertook this expedition under a flag of truce, and to violate that would expose us to capture or destruction by the British forces arrayed here in close proximity."

He pointed out at the bay where their ship lay, saying, "Even now, you can see that the British have moved one of their ships from its anchor by their fort, to stand guard over our little ship. We cannot offer any aid."

Lemuel nodded and said, "I understand that completely, and, for my part, I am happy to see the pursuit of knowledge proceeding without regard for the challenges of war. The matter of which I spoke, however, is but a trifle of transporting from these shores back to the friendlier ground of the American states a stranded Continental soldier and his daughter."

The student scowled for a moment, before answering, slowly, "We did carry three Loyalists from Boston hither, and I could, I suppose, speak to the master of the ship to see whether he would be willing to extend a similar courtesy to one of our own side." He shrugged. "So long as Colonel Campbell does not frustrate us in this matter, as he has in so many others, I can see no particular objection."

Lemuel made a sour face and said, "Well, that's just the trouble. The garrison is looking for this soldier—he stands accused of a crime—and so we would need to secret him among the crew, and keep his daughter out of sight entirely."

The student frowned deeply. "I will speak to the ship's master about it, but you ask us to take a serious risk on your behalf, one that could jeopardize the safety and scientific integrity of our expedition."

"Aye, I know, and I would not ask, but for the seriousness of the man's plight here."

"I can appreciate your eagerness to get a wanted man beyond the reach of the British who seek him, but I would not raise your hopes, only to dash them, should the ship's master decline to take the chance of discovery."

"I will await word of his decision, then." He straightened up as Doctor Williams passed near, within earshot. "Now, can I help you secure this canvas?"

The student nodded, and they lifted the wall of the tent into place, their discussions turning now to safer matters, as Lemuel asked him to describe the use of the various different instruments they had brought from the ship and arrayed around and within the barn.

"The entire intent of this expedition is to improve the knowledge of where, precisely, fixed points on the globe lie. If we know the exact latitude and longitude of a given point, we can determine where nearby settlements and so forth are located, so that when a ship is navigating over the sea, absent any sort of landmarks or waypoints, they can direct their rudder accurately to their destination nonetheless."

"I understand the importance of that, but the thing that I wondered at from the first moment that I heard speculation about this expedition was, simply, how does an eclipse help you to refine your knowledge of your location? As I conceive it, the eclipse happens, and then it's over, and you are still in the dark, if you will pardon the expression."

The student rewarded Lemuel's witticism with a chuckle, and then answered, "You understand what causes an eclipse of the sun?" Without waiting for confirmation, he held his fists out at arm's length, arranging them so that one cast a shadow on the other. "If the moon is this hand, and the earth this one, you can see that as the moon travels in its orbit around the earth, at certain times, it casts a shadow behind it, toward us."

Lemuel nodded, encouraging the student to continue. The student bobbed his head in enthusiasm and started to move the 'moon' fist around the 'earth' one in a circular motion. "Most of the time, that shadow misses the earth, as the moon's orbit is not exactly aligned with our orbit around the sun, so the shadow may pass above or below the earth."

"That makes sense, I suppose." Lemuel shivered slightly, adding, "It makes me feel strange to calmly discuss the moon moving about the earth in a circle like you're describing. I've always just thought of it as moving about the sky."

The student smiled at him and said, "But it is the very same thing, if you consider the viewpoint of a person at a fixed point, say, here"—he touched his finger to one of his knuckles—"and understand that the moon travels about the earth over the course of a month."

"Ah, so slowly; I was picturing the motion your hand described as taking place over a single night. That makes sense, then," Lemuel said. "Do carry on."

"I understand your confusion, and apologize for my lack of

clarity. Right, then, so sometimes, the moon's shadow passes above the earth, sometimes below. Now, the moon's shadow draws to a point, as we move further away from it. You've seen the same thing in shadows here, such as when the sun lies behind a tree, and you're in shade, but as you walk further and further away from the tree, the edge of the sun starts to show all around it."

Lemuel nodded in comprehension, and the student said, "The spot at which you first see the edge of the sun all around the tree is where the tree's shadow has come to a point. Most of the sun's light is blocked, but some of it is now reaching you from around the edges."

Looking skyward momentarily for emphasis, and still holding his fists so that one cast a shadow on the other, he continued, "Providence has placed the moon such that it is more common, when the earth does fall behind the moon's shadow, for the point of that shadow to fall just above our surface, and so we see the edges of the sun at all times throughout the eclipse."

"This eclipse, though, is one of the rare instances where the moon is a tiny bit closer to the earth at the moment when we pass behind it"—he moved his fists closer together to illustrate—"and so from our vantage here, the moon will cover the sun's face entirely."

"That is amazing," Lemuel remarked, shaking his head. "What a plan our Maker has, to present such wonders to us for our edification!"

The student smiled and nodded, saying, "So now, let me explain why this is important to being able to exactly calculate our position here."

He motioned to the clock, ticking away steadily beside the

wall. "You have seen the clock we brought here. It is probably the best clock in all of North America, having been purchased from the best clockmaker in London just before the war began. We will ensure over the next several days that it is exactly adjusted to local noon, by precisely measuring the sun's motion through the sky around mid-day."

"That sounds reasonable, but why is it so important to know the time?"

"Because, on the day of the eclipse, we will then be able to determine with great precision when specific parts of the event take place. With that knowledge, and some rigorous and painstaking mathematical analysis, which the good professor will doubtlessly suggest one of us would profit from performing on his behalf, we can calculate precisely where within the moon's shadow we stood when it crossed over our location."

"Ah, and with that knowledge, you can determine what your placement on the surface of the earth must have been?"

"Exactly, you have it. Now, Doctor Williams would have preferred a position a little further to the east or north, or both, as the center-line of the shadow passes through there, but according to the calculations he performed this afternoon, we should still be safely within the boundary of the shadow here, and of course, this wonderful barn and cleared fields give us advantages that any other location we could have reached lacked."

He scowled slightly through the back door of the barn, in the direction of the fort, and said, "Of course, too, this was the only place where our dear Colonel Campbell would permit us to land, as well. He has also informed us that we must depart immediately after the eclipse is over, which will deny us the chance to further refine the times provided by the clock, by ensuring that we have captured noon exactly on as many occasions as possible." He grimaced at the fog blanketing the landscape outdoors, adding, "This weather does not aid our efforts, either."

Lemuel nodded in agreement. "When these fogs appear, they can last for days." Seeing the look of panic that passed over the student's face, he added quickly, "'Tis but early in the season for that, though."

Changing the subject, he said, "'Tis a pity that the good colonel is so filled with distrust of your intentions here."

"Yes, it certainly is. We asked him to demonstrate that he is a friend of science, but he has at best shown that he is no more than tolerant of our efforts here. With such friends as he—and this fog—science should want little for enemies."

Chapter 27

The next day, another foggy one, though not as dense as the prior, George approached the student with whom he'd seen Lemuel speaking at length and introduced himself. "Ah, so you're the one to thank for this wonderfully clean place to work, then? I am John Davis, one of Doctor Williams' students, and I am pleased to make your acquaintance."

"I am glad to meet you, too, Mister Davis."

The student shook his head, saying, "Call me John, please."

"Thank you. My brother told me that you are very knowledgeable about the eclipse we are to see?"

"Aye, I am tolerably well-studied."

"What will it look like when it comes, then? Will it be akin to the darkness that passed over these parts this spring?"

"Nay, nothing like that." John said, leaning closer to speak in a low, conspiratorial tone. "Have a care in bringing up the topic of the Dark Day, though, as Doctor Williams and Mister Winthrop there suffered a very serious and public disagreement over its cause."

"Ah, then, I shall not mention it. But can you describe what we will see in the eclipse?"

"I cannot tell you from personal knowledge, no, but I can tell you what I have seen described in the proceedings recorded before several societies of natural philosophy, as I have read all such that I could lay my hands upon in preparation for this expedition."

George nodded, and John began. "At first, there will be little that you can see without you should have some special instruments such as we have carried here. As the eclipse nears its total phase, though, you will become sensible of the sky darkening, and if you should glance at the face of the sun, you would see that most all of it has vanished behind the moon."

John held his hand up at arm's length, and moved the other hand across it. "As the sun passes entirely behind the moon, you will see stars in the middle of the day, and your animals will act as though it were nightfall. You may feel the chill of night come over the air, and some observers have even recorded having seen great curtains of pale, pale light streaming out from behind the moon." He sighed, and added, "It is said to haunt the dreams of those who do see it for all their lives."

George narrowed his eyes, thinking of the darkness that spring. "And if there should be clouds, or this fog shall not have lifted?"

John chuckled humorlessly and answered, "Then you should see a great darkness pass over the faces of every member of the expedition, for our purpose in coming here will have been utterly thwarted by the caprices of the weather. Oh, you'd still see the day turned dark, and at the total phase, it would be as night, but you would not notice any of the more refined aspects of the eclipse."

"Well, then, I shall pray for a resumption of our fine weather of these recent days," George said, feeling vaguely sorry for even having asked the question.

"As shall we all," said John, laughing again. He looked

around, noting that there was nobody else within earshot. "Is your elder brother anywhere about? The master of our ship has some matters to discuss with him."

"Aye, I believe he is down at my father's house. I shall go and send him up."

"No, the master won't be up here, but may come to shore to consult with your brother."

"Then I shall tell Lemuel that."

"You will be doing your brother a service by delivering that message."

George smiled nervously at John and took his leave, passing Hiram and Alexander on their way up to the barn. They had been scarce the prior day, when there was work to be done, but they were overcome with curiosity now that the expedition had settled in.

George stopped to remonstrate them, "Mind that you don't disturb our guests, else Father will have your hides."

Hiram scowled at him, but Alexander scoffed, "And you'd know a thing or two about hides, wouldn't you? We'll not harass them as you have done, but are only going up to see what use they are making of our family's property."

George frowned at Alexander, but did not rise to the taunt, simply shaking his head and continuing down to the house. Since the abrupt end to his apprenticeship, Alexander seemed to take particular joy in trying to get a reaction out of George, teasing and prodding him at every opportunity. Their mother had noted the tension between them, and had quietly explained to George that his brother was likely jealous for the opportunity that had come his way, despite being the youngest of the brothers. In any event, there was nothing to be done for it but to shrug off his brother's occasional cruelty, and George had had years of experience at that.

He found Lemuel in the kitchen, eating a bowl of stew with their mother. George relayed the message he'd been given, and his brother leapt to his feet, saying, "I have been waiting for this conversation all day, Mother, so I will beg your forgiveness for my abrupt departure."

Their mother nodded tolerantly and said, "I have little doubt that your brother will be happy enough to finish your stew."

George sat down, saying, "As usual, Mother, you are correct." Lemuel laughed and rushed out the door.

George ate the abandoned stew, and he thought about what business Lemuel might have with the American ship's master, and he felt a chill descend over him as he realized what it must be. Putting down the spoon, he sighed deeply.

His mother gave him a puzzled look and said, "Whatever could draw such a sad sigh from you with so little outward warning?"

He sighed again, saying, "Well, you know Louise, right?"

"Aye, the girl that your brother brought in to help Beatrice around the house."

"The truth is, she is the same girl from the alley last spring, and her place in Lemuel's house has proven fortuitous to our friendship."

His mother smiled and said, "Did you think that your father and I were not aware of that fact? Indeed, we guessed that your brother was also aware of it, and that it was the reason for having her come to help Beatrice, in addition to wanting to care for his wife and daughter."

George felt his face flush, but he ploughed on, saying, "It is likely that she will accompany her father back to Boston on board the American ship, if Lemuel can arrange for it. If that should happen, then I will never again see her."

His mother frowned and nodded slowly. "That is reason enough for a sigh, George." She sighed herself, and said, "As a mother, I want to protect my boys from the sad realities of the world, but there always comes a day when I am powerless to do so. I am sorry that this is one of those days."

She stood and came around to the side of the table where George sat, beckoning him to her. He rose and let her gather him into his arms for a long moment.

Finally, he pulled away and said, "I may well be making more out of all of this than it merits. She is, after all, but a friend, and we do not yet even know whether their passage will be arranged. It is too early to mourn something that may not even merit mourning anyway."

He shrugged, still bearing a miserable expression on his face. "I only wish that I could control what my heart wants. She kisses my cheek, though, and I lose all track of what I was trying to control, and just want to feel that way all the time."

"You are no different from any other young man in love, George, and I would expect no less of you."

He gave her a look of horror, retorting, "I said nothing of love, Mother, only that she is a friend."

His mother smiled tolerantly and said, "Friends do not usually kiss one another, nor do they pine so deeply at the prospect of being parted. You are blessed—and cursed—with the same heart that I had to endure in my youth; indeed that I still endure even today. You feel things more deeply than do your brothers, which is a grand thing when it comes to love, and a terrible thing when you are faced with loss."

She pulled her son into her arms again, stroking the top of his head and slowly rocking him back and forth. "You are extraordinarily lucky to be learning the lessons of the heart so young, and while you still have many years in which to find a path that will bring you joy in the end."

Muffled against her shoulder, he said, "I don't feel very lucky. I feel the exact opposite of lucky." He stood back again and said, "Mother, she could choose to stay . . . but she's choosing her father over me. That doesn't sound very much like there is any sort of love between me and her, does it?"

His mother looked thoughtful, and answered, "Choosing between what your family wants of you, and what your heart desires is never easy, George. When your father proposed coming here, leaving everything we knew and were comfortable with to try our luck in a new place, where we could have the land we wanted, build the house we needed, and live the life we chose . . . my parents were deeply opposed to it."

She looked off into the distance, her eyes bright with remembered pain. "My father went so far as to say that he would forget that he even had a daughter, if I were to follow my husband here to the frontiers of the colony. He didn't think that he could stand the worry about my safety here, and he did not trust in your father's ability to provide an adequate home for me."

She turned back to meet George's eyes, saying, "When I boarded the ship to come here with my husband, your grandfather did not even come to the docks to say farewell, and I never saw him again."

She gestured with her hands, adding, "Of course, once your father and I were established here, I did restore correspondence with your grandfather, and we came to better understand each other . . . but when I got word that he had died, the first thing that I remembered was the awful feeling of watching the dock fall out of view, without him there to say good-bye to me."

Just then, Lemuel came through the door, looking drawn and weary. George looked at him intently, an unspoken question in his eyes. Lemuel said, "George, I must speak to you in private for a moment," and gestured with his head for his brother to follow him out into the bright sunshine.

Giving his mother a last squeeze, he went to the door, dreading what his brother would tell him. "You spoke to the ship's master?"

Lemuel nodded slowly. "Aye, I talked the master of the *Lincoln* into taking our friend back to Boston, posing as a crew member, so as to avoid detection by the British garrison."

He sighed, saying, "However, the master refused to take Louise, as he could think of no way to explain her presence on board to any patrol that might stop and search the ship on the way back home. If Mister Johnson goes, his daughter must stay here."

Chapter 28

"It is beyond civilized consideration, and that is the end of it," said Mister Johnson, his arms crossed before him. "I will leave no daughter of mine behind, unaccompanied, to find what fate has in store for her absent the counsel and guidance of a father."

Louise gritted her teeth, answering, "Dad, it is beyond civilized consideration that you should stay here one day beyond what you must, trusting to dumb chance whether someone should happen to spot you emptying a chamber pot or calling for me at the door. While there are not many on this island, we don't know whether all are friendly to our cause, and it takes but one offhand remark, one innocent question, to set into motion a chain of events that can end only with you at the end of a hangman's rope."

She crossed her own arms and glared fiercely at her father. "I'll not see you swing on my account, and most particularly not when you know me to be capable of looking after myself."

"You are still just a girl, Louise, and this place is afflicted with a British garrison whose troops are known to not always conduct themselves as gentlemen." He gave Lemuel a significant glance, and the other man's mouth compressed into a grim, tight line.

"No girl alone here, particularly one who is kin to a known, wanted rebel agitator and killer, will be safe among this community without a man shall accompany her at all times."

Louise shot George a demanding look and said, "George, shall you tell my Dad again about the day we met?"

George shifted uncomfortably from one foot to the other. He'd purposely made himself inconspicuous in the corner of the room, and Lemuel was similarly situated in the opposite corner, still looking angry both at the memory of Beatrice's ordeal, and that the rebel soldier had brought up the memory of it.

Mister Johnson said quickly, "That won't be necessary, George. I have heard several accounts on my daughter's actions that day." He gave Louise a reproachful look. "You are lucky indeed that the man whom you injured was unwilling to admit that he'd been so beaten by a girl, else we might be worried about whether the garrison would be seeking justice against you, instead."

He shook his head. "Nay, I do not worry about whether you have the ability to defend yourself, but I do believe that my work in providing a moderating influence over the passions that rule your heart is unfinished."

He grimaced and added, "Nor is it likely to ever be finished, until you shall have a husband upon whom to expend your energies."

Louise's eyes narrowed into a glare, and for a moment, she seemed to be about to explode in fury. Her expression turned suddenly calculating, and an odd little smile played at the corner of her mouth. Then, she turned suddenly to George, saying, "Do you think, Mister Williams, that you are equal to the job of, as my dear father puts it, 'moderating' my passions?"

George inhaled sharply as he realized what Louise was driving at, and he could feel his face burn as though it were consumed in flame. At the same time, he could see that her father had blanched white. George managed to sputter, "You—you can't mean what it sounds as though you are suggesting!"

"I can, and I am. George Williams, will you marry me?"

A long, long silence fell over the room in the wake of Louise's question, and George found that though he could feel his pulse racing, his thoughts seemed to be moving more slowly than molasses. Louise wanted to stay here with him—forever!—which made his heart leap with joy, but marriage . . . marriage was for life, and the implications of being wed brought a fresh flush to his face.

He was aware of the moments of silence building upon themselves, one upon the next, and knew, too, that a question such as this was not one to be answered thoughtlessly, but too long a delay was an answer of its own sort. With that realization, his considerations became much more clear, and he looked into her eyes and answered, solemnly, "I would be most honored, Louise, if your father will give his approval to our union."

Mister Johnson had been stricken mute, himself, at Louise's proposal, and George watched, fascinated in spite of himself, as a vein popped up along the side of the man's forehead, visibly pulsing with his heartbeat. He took a deep breath, and then seemed to shrink down into himself a bit as he answered quietly, "George is a good man. If this is what your heart truly wants, my daughter, I shall not stand in your way."

George blinked as Louise threw her arms about him fiercely, and he was shocked to feel tears where her face pressed against his neck. She said, with a catch in her voice, "I had hoped that we might have had the opportunity to court more properly, and observe all of the proper forms in coming to this moment, but I knew from our first meeting that I wanted you for my husband, George."

He returned her embrace, saying, "I dared not to hope nor even dream of such, but I am grateful beyond measure at this outcome, Louise." Raising his eyes from her hair, he caught her father's eye over her shoulder and added, "I shall endeavor to provide for your daughter, sir, and I will see to her safety in these times, ahead of any other worldly concern."

Mister Johnson nodded gravely to George. "I have all confidence that you will prove equal to that, and I wish you the joy of a long and happy union."

He took his daughter's shoulder and gently turned her around to face him. "I called you a mere girl a moment ago, and it seems that I may have, once more, underestimated you."

He smiled ruefully. "I ought know by now that I do so at my own peril, but I sometimes forget that you are more like your mother than the little girl I bounced on my knee. I knew that the day would come when you departed my house to make your own family, but I never suspected that permitting you to accompany me here would bring it to pass even sooner than nature would have it do." Blinking back a tear, he murmured, almost to himself, "How is it that you have grown to womanhood so quickly?"

"Oh, Daddy," Louise said, and rushed into her father's arms now, tears streaming openly down her face. "It is not the place, nor that you brought me here, that hastened this. 'Tis but happy fortune that brought George and I together, and I'll not have you reproach yourself for that."

Lemuel spoke up now from the other side of the room. "Father and Mother will, I am certain, give their blessing to your union as well, though they will be most startled at the speed with which you have arranged it." He nodded sagely, with a small twinkle in his eye, adding, "Not so startled as will be our brothers, though."

George began to laugh at that thought, and found that he could hardly stop laughing, as all of the tension and anxiety that he had been holding within in the days since he had found his master's lifeless corpse seemed determined to escape all at once.

He was aware of Lemuel regarding him quizzically, and of Louise and her father exchanging nervous smiles, as the laughter continued to bubble up out of him. He would just begin to regain control of himself when he would picture Hiram's or Alexander's face at hearing the news, and another fit of giggles would arise.

Finally, Louise put her hand on his shoulder, concern on her face, and said, "Are you all right, dear George?"

He could feel the steadiness of her presence through her hand, and he drew a deep, shuddering breath, nodding, and saying, "Aye. I am, now."

Chapter 29

Although Helen wanted her son to have "a proper wedding," Shubael overrode her, pointing out that they could hardly ask Colonel Campbell to conduct the ceremony, nor could they ask Mister Johnson to forgo his passage from the British-held territory.

In the end, Lemuel resolved the problem, slipping away and returning with the master of the *Lincoln* in tow. A stubborn, gruff, but not hard-hearted man, Captain Mowett had agreed to perform the marriage, though he took pains to make clear that he would not be able to record it in his log so as to avoid revealing his cooperation with the rebels.

George's mother had to settle for hurriedly brushing and braiding Louise's hair into a gorgeous arrangement atop the girl's head before the two young people stood before the officer and repeated the graven words after him.

"I, George, take thee, Louise . . . "

". . . in sickness and in health . . . "

". . . 'til death do us part."

When it was over, and the blush from kissing a girl—his wife!—in front of everyone had faded, George and Louise sat quietly while their families chattered in happy shock around them.

"Louise, I . . . this doesn't seem real."

"Nor to me, dear George, but I am glad that I may now

profess my love without feeling as though I am in danger of a sin."

George smiled gently. "Sin, Louise?"

It was her turn to blush, and she looked away.

"Never mind that now; there can be no sin between us now, and my father sails to safety with the expedition just two days hence."

"So soon? The eclipse is supposed to happen just tomorrow, and the student I spoke with had said that he should very much like to have as much as a month of observations to be certain of the adjustments on their clock."

"Aye, that accursed Colonel Campbell has issued orders that they must raise anchor the very next day, out of fear that they might yet become embroiled in some rebel plot."

She gave him an impish smile and added, "Can you even imagine that these natural philosophers would turn from their studies to involve themselves in the matters of the mundane world?"

George smiled back and took her hand. "Your father told me that he planned to return with the captain to the ship after supper, so as to become acquainted with the duties that will attend his position there. Ruse or no, he means to work alongside the men of the ship to earn his passage."

She nodded, saying, "Of course."

George continued, "Lemuel offered us the use of the spare room you two have been using, until we can get a house raised." He blushed yet again and added, "Lemuel said that the walls are thick, and we need not fear hearing him and Beatrice, though the baby may wake us."

She smiled at him, squeezing his fingers in her hand, and saying, "I am certain that we will manage. It is most kind of your brother to extend his hospitality even further."

Gesturing through the window, he said, "Father said that we shall have the back portion of the north end of the farm as a wedding gift, and Hiram and Alexander are already making plans for a house raising." He frowned slightly and said, almost more to himself, "I don't know what malady they may be suffering, for they have both been suddenly taken with being kind to me, without explanation."

She got a faraway look in her eye, saying, "I suppose we shall have a farm of our own, then, and not live in town."

"Aye, with my apprenticeship broken, and my training so far from complete, there are not many other options open to us."

She nodded. "No matter, we shall make a success of it, I doubt not. I do miss the society of such friends as I had in the village, but I expect that I shall see them often enough."

"I will see to it, so long as your safety is not compromised in the doing."

She fixed him with a sour look, and he smiled in answer. "Aye, I know that you are full capable of looking after yourself, but you must allow me to at least observe the proper forms of seeing to my wife's security."

Her frown turned to a wry smile, and she said, "I will do my best to permit you to attend to your duties to me . . . but I am accustomed to seeing to things myself." She gave him a dangerous look, leavened with a twinkle in her eye, and added, "Do not forget that I am a notorious rebel spy, after all, and have even gone so far as to conduct a night-time raid on a British fort. I am unlikely to be satisfied with any silk-lined prison, when the big, wild world beckons without."

He smiled and took her hand, pressing it to his lips. "I

am unlikely to forget, and should I suffer any momentary lapse in memory, I trust that you will remind me with more gentleness than I have seen you sometimes exhibit."

She shook her head and rolled her eyes at him, a grin stealing over her face in answer. Lemuel sauntered over then, with Beatrice beside him, the baby swaddled securely in her arms. Though she had dark circles under her eyes, George had never seen his brother's wife look happier, and he took her proffered hand in both of his warmly as she said quietly, "I give you joy of your marriage, George, and I am pleased beyond words to welcome your wife into our family permanently."

"Thank you, Beatrice," he replied.

Louise added, "I am overjoyed that these late upsets have reached such a happy resolution, and I cannot express my gratitude for your hospitality while we work to set up our own housekeeping."

Beatrice smiled, saying, "'Tis nothing, my sister Louise. Once you do have your own home, I will be glad for the opportunity to help you establish yourself there as well. I have a sourdough that my mother gave to me, and which I would be most happy to share with you in turn."

Lemuel silently embraced George and, for once, seemed at a loss for words, just giving his brother a couple of thumps on the back before releasing him and hurrying away with his family. George wondered at it all as he watched Lemuel cross the room and quickly pour himself a large mug of cider. Lemuel struck dumb, and his other brothers kind? The world had truly turned upside-down.

Chapter 30

The first rays of dawn crept across the bed over the sill of his window, and slowly passed across George's eyes. He groaned, rolling over to shade his face. His eyes flew open as he found that he was not alone in the bed, and even as his heart abandoned racing from surprise, it began anew as he remembered all that had passed the prior day.

Louise did not stir, but slumbered on, her face relaxed and soft in the morning light. George had to remind himself that this was no dream, that he was, in fact, married to this vision of soft cheeks, downy lashes, and delicate whorl of an ear, half-covered with the wild hair of morning.

He was still gazing at her, a gentle smile on his lips, when the sun reached her face, and she cracked open one eye to see him there. She closed her eye again, and murmured, "What are staring at, my husband?"

"Only the most beautiful vision I could ever hope to behold," he answered, and leaned forward to brush his lips against her forehead. "We must be up and to our tasks, though—the eclipse is mere hours hence, and I expect that you should like what time you can find to farewell your father as well."

Her eyes still closed, she answered, "How is it that I did not inquire to learn that you were one of those who greets the morning with eager discussion, while we civilized folk keep our silence until the warm humours of the day have had an opportunity to bring us to full wakefulness?"

She opened one eye and gave him a mock frown, the shook her head and rose on one elbow to kiss him briefly, before rolling away and flipping the blankets off herself to stand. As she stretched, George admired the graceful curve of her neck, and permitted himself a brief remembrance of holding her in his arms as they'd drifted off to sleep.

Sighing, he swung his legs over the side of the bed and rose, himself. "Most mornings, my dear, I will be content to grant you the peace of a quiet morning, but today, I wish to shout from the rooftops." He grinned widely at her, and she returned his smile wryly, shaking her head.

"I can forgive you that urge today, for I feel it, too." She frowned, suddenly, and added more somberly, "I only wish that Daddy were not so abruptly leaving these shores. 'Tis the one dark place in an otherwise sunny day."

George walked around the bed and took her hands in his own, saying, "I know, Louise, and I wish that there were some other option open to him. We cannot choose the circumstances of our world, but can only work to improve them." He grimaced, and added, "Or, at least, undertake to do those things which we believe will improve our circumstances."

She nodded, her gaze distant and thoughtful, and he drew her into an embrace. After a moment, he stepped back and gestured through the window. "'Tis not the only darkness that will visit this day. The eclipse is foretold mere hours hence."

"Aye," she said, her voice still soft and sad from the melancholy prospect of what the morrow must inevitably bring.

"We ought bring the men of the expedition some sustenance—they will doubtless have no thought for such as they conduct their philosophical observations."

"'Tis a thoughtful gesture, and one that they will doubtless appreciate. I'll . . . step out of the room so that you may dress." George blushed, and then shook his head, an embarrassed smile growing over his face. Louise smiled slowly back at him, and he opened the door, slipping out into the front room.

There, Lemuel was just bringing in a load of wood for the morning fire, and Beatrice stood at the hearth, the baby balanced on her hip. Lemuel looked over his shoulder at George, grinning at the long nightshirt his brother still wore. He spared George any teasing, merely nodding in greeting, though his eyes danced brightly with unspoken mirth.

"Good morning, George," said Beatrice quietly. "I trust that the baby did not disturb you?"

"Nay," George replied, "I heard nothing, and slept better than I ever did in my own bed." He refused to acknowledge his burning face, maintaining a steady gaze as he spoke to his sister-in-law.

She smiled gently and said, "I am glad to hear it. Would you hold Constance for a bit, that I may prepare our breakfast?"

"Surely," he said, and she handed the child over to him. Though swaddled as usual, Constance's eyes were alert and wide open as she took in the sight of an unfamiliar face looming over her. Her reaction hung in the balance between startled delight and fearful tears, but George's friendly smile triggered a cherubic grin in return.

George was still trading smiles with his niece when Louise

emerged from the room, properly dressed for the day. She and Beatrice immediately busied themselves at the hearth, leaving George dandling the baby. Looking out through the window at the barn, he could see John busying himself with the instruments, sighting down the tube of one, scribbling down notes, then hurrying to the next.

While George could not see the sun from where he sat, he could already sense the young natural philosopher's growing excitement at the observations to come. Doctor Williams emerged from the barn, looking as though he had not so much as bothered to have drawn a comb through his wild hair—or, if he had, his nervous habit of running his hand through it had by now utterly undone his customary neat appearance. He conferred briefly with the younger man, nodded briskly, and positioned himself at the eyepiece of the telescope, peering intently at the sun through it.

John had explained to George that this would ordinarily be a means of utterly blinding oneself, but they had taken the precaution of stacking several plates of glass before the front lens of the telescope, each of which had been carefully smoked over a candle flame, resulting in a nearly opaque barrier to the sun's rays.

"Concentrated as they are by the instrument, the light of the sun is powerful enough to set a candle aflame, and Doctor Williams assures me that it remains so even at the very most extreme stages of the eclipse, until it is obscured entirely by the moon. If we do not wish to risk instant blindness, we must take these precautions to preserve our sight."

George had nodded, remembering how, as a young child, he had stared steadfastly one evening at the setting sun for several minutes, and had been unable to see anything in the spot where the sun's image had been for the remainder of the evening. He could only imagine how much more extreme the phenomenon would be through the lenses of the powerful telescopes that the expedition had fetched here with them.

Doctor Williams suddenly glanced away from the eyepiece to the great clock, which sat inside the doorway of the barn, and made a hurried notation at the portable table set up beside the gleaming instrument. Within seconds, the other men who were gazing through telescopes were following suit, and a ripple of low comments passed among them. Doctor Williams made a sharp comment, and the natural philosophers and laborers alike turned to their assigned tasks. From all of this, George surmised that the long-anticipated event had finally begun, and darkness would shortly fall once again in the midst of daylight.

Unlike the previous instance, however, the sky was nearly free of cloud today, although the morning's frost whitened the ground still shadowed from the sun. "I think," said George, "that I should go and dress, as it appears that it may soon be worthwhile to venture out of doors to witness the spectacle."

Louise frowned at George, saying, "Can it not wait until Beatrice and I are finished here?"

Beatrice smiled at her and said, "It is of no concern, sister. Go and take the babe and let your husband do as he sees necessary."

Louise gave a weary sigh, but her smile to George as she accepted the now-giggling baby from him was patient and playful. "Go, then, my husband, and behold the spectacle that promises to transform our world for this day. We shall feed you with the others, if you like."

George kissed her cheek as he passed her. "Thank you,

Louise, for tolerating my enthusiasm in this."

As he hurried to the bedroom, Lemuel called out to him quietly, with a teasing smirk, "I hope you are equally enthusiastic in other matters, my brother."

His face burning red, George grimaced and escaped the kitchen, pulling the bedroom door closed behind him.

Once dressed, he hurried out to the vicinity of the barn, although he paused at a distance from the laboring philosophers so as not to distract them from their appointed tasks. John glanced up, nodded quickly to him in acknowledgement of his presence, and returned to scribbling notes on the large ledger-book that laid open on his table.

George was startled when the philosopher John had introduced as Professor Sewall called out in a low voice, "Should you like to see the specter of our sun giving the appearance of having had a bite taken out of his limb, son?" The intensity and fierce concentration that George had seen in the days of preparation seemed to have relented for a moment, and the man seemed composed, even nearly relaxed.

Regaining his own composure, George answered, "I would like nothing better, sir, so long as I am not disrupting your studies."

Sewall leaned back in the low chair he had placed before the telescope's eye piece. "'Tis no disruption; we have timed the first phenomenon of the eclipse, I am not due to record my next observation for a few minutes hence. Come, take a look."

George approached the gleaming brass instrument—longer than his arm, and, he thought, probably worth more—cautiously, as though his breath alone could disrupt the device. Professor Sewall rose from his chair and motioned for George to take his place. George ignored the envious glances the professor's companions directed at him, and sat where he was told.

Placing his hand on George's shoulder, the older man pointed into the end of the eye piece, saying, "You will look through here, and you may behold the sight I have described to you. Have a care to not nudge the telescope, lest you lose the sun in its view."

George craned his neck to position his eye as Professor Sewall directed, moving his head about as he caught a glimpse of light through the glass. He closed his other eye reflexively, so as to focus his attention on the view through the eye-piece, shifting until he found just the right spot, and the image revealed itself to his vision.

He gasped in spite of himself—the brilliant orange disk that he saw did, indeed, give the appearance of having been bitten into, a smooth, circular portion of it blacked out along one edge, forming what looked like a dent or—yes—a bite taken out of the edge. He could see several smudges darkening the face of the sun, but he could not tell if they were a flaw of the instrument through which he was looking, or a flaw in the heretofore perfect disk of the sun. Still gazing through the telescope, he asked, "That is truly the moon beginning to pass before the sun, then?"

"Aye, 'tis, and I see that you've been paying close attention to the lessons these boys give out to all who will hold still long enough to hear them." George could hear the smile in the man's voice, though he could not pull himself away from the view to verify that the stern natural philosopher had, indeed, grinned.

The hand on George's shoulder squeezed briefly, and the doctor said, "Right, then, that's enough; I must return to my post and record what I can of the other phenomena attendant to the eclipse."

Reluctantly, George looked away from the eye piece, his vision still dazzled in the eye he had been using. He blinked hard, and saw John looking away, a smirk on his face. George stood, still shaking his head in wonder, and turned to face Professor Sewall.

"Sir, I thank you most sincerely for permitting me to partake in this wonder," he said quietly, so as not to be heard by the others. "It was an un-looked-for opportunity, and one that I will not soon forget."

The corners of Sewall's eyes crinkled in the approximation of a smile, and he said to the younger man, "The best of the event is yet to come, my friend. You'll not need any fancy equipment to perceive it, either, if what I have heard reported of these spectacles holds true."

George nodded and backed out of the professor's path to his chair, saying, "I am filled with anticipation, and have many more questions I should like to pose to you, but I do not wish to distract you further from your interrogation of the sky."

Again, Sewall nearly smiled, and he said, "Aye, there may be time for questions later, though, should you come around after the eclipse has ended." He resumed his seat and returned to the eye piece of the telescope, reaching up to make a small adjustment to the instrument. He took up his pen and scribbled down some further notes, and George could tell that the natural philosopher was no longer even aware of his presence, so he retreated to stand near a corner of the barn.

John nodded to him with something akin to respect, and George felt for a moment as though he were, in some small way, a member of this august company of philosophers.

    The feeling was shattered by his brother touching his elbow, unseen as he'd approached, causing George to lurch into the wall clumsily in surprise. Lemuel sniggered quietly and whispered, "If your ponderings of nature may be interrupted, Beatrice and Louise should like your assistance in carrying breakfast out to the men." Once George's heart had stopped racing at the surprise of Lemuel's appearance, he nodded and followed his brother back to the house.

Chapter 31

Though the natural philosophers expressed their appreciation for the plates laden with bread, cheese, and fruit that George helped the women carry out to them, none paid the food much attention, as they were each occupied with their instruments, notes, and even sketches of what they were seeing through their eyepieces.

George stood for a while at the periphery of the barn, looking out over the landscape, Louise at his side. While nothing had seemed particularly out of the ordinary when Professor Sewall had given him a glance through his telescope, George could now perceive that the light of the late morning was taking on a peculiar cast—as though a cloud sat before the sun, though the sky was blue and clear, and there was only a bit of haze visible over the mainland in the distance. Too, the color of the sky itself seemed to be darkening as though evening approached, regardless of the fact that the sun still climbed into the sky.

He walked over to where Professor Sewall bent to his eyepiece, and asked quietly, "How much longer now, sir?"

Sewall looked up with a distracted smile and answered, "Not long now, I should not expect. The greater portion of the sun is now obscured, and the whole shadow of the moon is close upon us." He returned to his eyepiece, the notepaper beside him seemingly forgotten as he absorbed the spectacle the instrument revealed to him.

The shade of blue in the sky grew deeper by the moment, and George felt a chill settle over him. He could see birds flocking into the nearby trees, and the cock crowed to draw the hens of his harem to the safety of their roost. Along the ridgeline, George saw the cows streaming back toward his brother's barn, where they had already become accustomed to being kept for the duration of the philosophers' visit.

And yet, with all of these signs of the approaching darkness, George could feel his breakfast still warm in his belly, and when he walked back over to take Louise's hand, he felt none of the weariness of a long day's work.

Doctor Williams was in constant motion now, making minute adjustments at his telescope, calling out a stream of figures for his assistant to take down in a neat, careful hand, and glancing back and forth between the eyepiece and the clock. With every jump of the second hand, the sky became more ominous, and the tension around the barn grew higher.

Louise made a quiet exclamation and gripped George's arm, pointing over toward the British fortification across the bay. Above it in the sky, a bright star had appeared in the darkening sky, and Sewall, hearing her, looked up, followed her finger to the spark in the sky, and nodded knowingly.

"Venus," he said quietly, with a small, enigmatic smile, and again returned to his eyepiece.

Louise frowned, saying wonderingly into George's ear, "I spied Venus at dawn yesterday, and it faded from view as the sun rose . . . and yet, here it appears again at mid-day."

He replied back into her ear, "Yet more wonders await, if

these fellows are to be believed."

Still the sky darkened, and more stars appeared in the gloaming, though still not so many as at true night.

Sewall had now sat back from his telescope, and peered through a smoked glass directly up at the sun. George squinted up at it as well, and while he could perceive that the familiar orb was greatly diminished by the passage of the moon before it, he could see only that it formed a crescent still.

One of the students likewise peered through a piece of smoked glass, and was scowling mightily as he scrawled notes on the paper before him. He glanced over at Doctor Williams as if in preparation to say something, shook his head, and returned to looking through the glass, shaking his head as if in disbelief.

Finally, the student said something quiet and urgent to Williams, who scowled in reply and returned to his eyepiece yet again. Even as George watched the natural philosopher's shoulders fall, he thought he could sense the light increasing.

More of the observers were frowning and muttering to one another, and finally, George could bear it no longer. "Professor Sewall, what is the matter?"

Sewall looked away from his eyepiece to regard George with now-saddened eyes. He said, quietly and precisely, "There has been some mistake; this was not a total eclipse, at least not in this location."

Williams whirled and glared at Sewall. "There has been no mistake," he said fiercely. "That thrice-damned British colonel has doomed our expedition hence to failure and ruin, out of a short-sighted demand that we set up operations far from where I had hoped, and outside the zone of totality."

He spat on the floor of the barn, adding, "This accursed war has spoilt months of preparation, and set back the advance of science and navigation by untold years." Eyes narrowing, he added in Louise's direction, "I hope that you and your allies are well-satisfied." Louise gasped and covered her mouth in surprise at his venom, and George took a step forward, intent on making the man retract his poisonous words.

Louise pulled him back to her side, and Williams turned his back on everyone present, returning to his eyepiece and again barking out figures for his hapless assistant to write down. Other than the ticking of the clock, there was no other sound for many long minutes, until George gathered Louise under his arm and led her back down to the house, shaking with indignation and anger.

Chapter 32

The departure of the expedition the next day was a somber affair. As the students and crew of the ship disassembled and carted away the delicate instruments, Doctor Williams stood at the top of the bluff facing the British fort with his arms crossed, glaring daggers at the object of his anger. Nobody disturbed him until the last item was stowed in the hold of the *Lincoln*, the last provisions carried aboard, and the final farewells were being exchanged.

As the leader of the expedition passed, Louise's father, now dressed as an ordinary seaman with a coarse knit cap pulled over his brow, found her and George on the shore where the ship's launches were drawn up. His eyes were rimmed in red, but he betrayed no emotion as he took George by the shoulders, looking his son-in-law steadily in the eye.

"You'll take care of her, and keep her safe." It was not a request or a query, but a flat statement.

"Of course, sir," the younger man replied. Johnson nodded, briefly embraced him, and then turned to his daughter.

"You'll take care of him, and keep him safe." Louise nodded quickly, tears pouring down her face, and pulled her father into tight, wordless embrace.

After a long moment, she released him, replying firmly, "You'll take care of yourself, Daddy, and keep yourself safe."

Her father nodded, his own eyes brimming with tears, and then he turned and joined the rest of the men accompanying Doctor Williams back to the boat.

George wrapped his arm around Louise's shoulder, breathing in time with her, as the launch pulled away from the shore and back to the waiting *Lincoln*.

As the sails on the American vessel rose up to meet the evening breeze, the couple walked up to the top of the bluff, and together they watched it sail out of the bay and into the soft indigo darkness of the evening.

Also in Audiobook

Many readers love the experience of turning the pages in a paper book such as the one you hold in your hands. Others enjoy hearing a skilled narrator tell them a story, bringing the words on the page to life.

Brief Candle Press has arranged to have *The Darkness* produced as a high-quality audiobook, and you can listen to a sample and learn where to purchase it in that form by scanning the QR code below with your phone, tablet, or other device, or going to the Web address shown.

Happy listening!

bit.ly/TheDarknessAudio

Historical Notes

T he convulsions of a new nation's birth may throw into disarray all of the normal matters of civil life, but the opportunities for astronomical observations cannot generally be rearranged for the convenience of mortal men.

The eclipse of 1780 offered, as described, a chance to refine the calculations of longitude, which would have benefitted both civil and military uses. The Continental Congress, having been persuaded of this fact by the tireless Doctor Williams, directed its president—the infamous John Hancock—to send a letter to the British occupiers of the territory over which the eclipse would appear.

That letter offers a fascinating glance into the place that the new United States hoped to occupy in relation to its mother country, as well as a look at the operations of scientific inquiry during the war.

The eclipse expedition unfolded roughly as depicted, though the names of Shubael's family members are not prominent in the histories that survive. The expedition was, indeed, considered to have been a failure, and that failure was due either to a miscalculation on Doctor Williams' part, the restrictions placed on his movements by the British, or a combination of the two.

One of the great ironies, however, is that Doctor Williams recorded a phenomenon that was apparently previously unknown to science—namely, the brilliant "beads" of light that appear along the limb of the moon's shadow, as sunlight streams through valleys between the mountains along the edge of its disk. Those droplets of light are clearly visible in a sketch that Doctor Williams made of the eclipse, and prominently described in his report on the event.

However, it was a later (British) scientist who would grasp what caused the phenomenon, which is named for him today, called "Bailey's Beads."

The unsettling and strange "Dark Day" that affected the same area (and, indeed, a much larger area than the eclipse) happened earlier in the same year, and is documented as described, including the sort of speculations as to its cause shown in the excerpt included in the text of this book.

It is now believed to have been caused by inland forest fires, a theory that is strengthened by the widespread descriptions of a burning smell and ashfall in its wake.

That both of these events should have taken place within the span of a few months is a great coincidence, and while neither had any direct bearing on the outcome of the war, both contributed to the widespread sense of unease and fear that overshadowed the middle years of the conflict, when the outcome was far from certain, and the American Revolution gave every appearance of being ready to slip into history's shadows.

Acknowledgements

Every book I write is informed by great piles of research performed by hundreds of years of academics who have preceeded me. In the case of this book, though, the dedication of one researcher—Robert Friend Rothschild—in compiling his excellent biography of Samuel Williams, *Two Brides for Apollo*, was simply indispensible. Williams was a hugely influential scientist and academic in his own right, and I am richer for having learned so much about him from Rothschild's book.

Thanks, too, to my friend Sean League of Vixen Optics, who is an expert in equipment used for solar observation, for suggesting that a stack of smoked glass would have been the most likely means used by the Williams expedition to attenuate the sun's rays for telescopic observation. It is one of the few details of the expedition's outfitting that was not well-documented in the sources that I could locate.

Finally, I'd like to acknowledge the substantial contributions of my editor, Ingrid Bevz of Green Ink Proofreading, whose many helpful suggestions and corrections improved this novel greatly. After working through her edits to this novel, I am going to find a way to make my computer beep at me every time I use a comma. Any errors, of course, remain my own.

Thank You

I deeply appreciate you spending the past couple of hundred pages with the characters and events of a world long past, yet hopefully relevant today.

If you enjoyed this book, I'd also be grateful for a kind review on your favorite bookseller's Web site or social media outlet. Word of mouth is the best way to make me successful, so that I can bring you even more high-quality stories of bygone times.

I'd love to hear directly from you, too—feel free to reach out to me via my Facebook page, Twitter feed, or Web site and let me know what you liked, and what you would like me to work on more.

Again, thank you for reading, for telling your friends about this book, for giving it as a gift or dropping off a copy in your favorite classroom or library. With your support and encouragement, we'll find even more times and places to explore together.

larsdhhedbor.com
Facebook: LarsDHHedbor
@LarsDHHedbor on Twitter

Enjoy a preview of the next book in the
Tales From a Revolution series:

<u>The Path</u>

The grass in the field was as high as Yves' hip, and was dry enough to rustle loudly as he moved through it. He held his musket before him as he walked slowly, half-crouched and trying to move slowly enough that he would make no sound, despite the dry grass. He held his musket at the ready, with the pan primed and the bore packed with an innovative load that the Americans were fond of, consisting of a standard ball, preceded out of the muzzle by several small buckshot pellets.

Gerard had urged him to try the new load, saying, "General Washington insists that all of his troops load this way. They call it 'buck and ball,' and it's said to increase the likelihood of striking your target significantly."

"But can the buckshot stop a target as well as a ball?"

"No, but it's better than a miss."

Yves had nodded thoughtfully and had taken a handful of the premade paper cartridges Gerard had offered. Now, out in the field, he had torn the back off one with his teeth, primed the pan and dropped the rest of the cartridge down the barrel of his musket, following it with the ramrod, which he used to gently tamp the load down firmly into place at the back of his gun's barrel.

His musket was prepared, then, as he saw a rustling in the grass ahead of him. He did not hear his quarry's telltale sound, but he could now see the grass moving about, perhaps thirty yards away.

Moving very deliberately, he brought the musket to his shoulder and sighted down the barrel at the point at which he anticipated that his target would appear. He took a deep, calming breath, his finger sliding inside the loop that protected the trigger and resting on the fatal bit of metal gently.

As he expected, a group of geese burst up from the ground, taking flight and presenting a multitude of targets, wheeling into the sky. Yves pulled the trigger and over the deafening roar of the gun firing by his ear, he thought he heard the high-pitched shriek of . . . a girl?

Two of the geese he had fired at faltered and dropped to the ground, with distinct thumps. It sounded as though one still had some fight in it, honking and struggling in the grass, but the other made no sound at all. Between Yves and where the bird lay, though, a head popped up, dark of hair and skin and the look of utter terror in her eyes made the horse seller's slave girl all but unrecognizable at first. She looked at Yves and the terror on her face gave way to recognition, and her shoulders slumped as she sighed audibly in what sounded to Yves like resignation.

She lifted her hands into the air, tears streaming down her cheeks and she called out, in her oddly-accented French. "Please don't shoot, monsieur. I do not want to return to my master, but I want to live, even . . . even if it means going back."

Yves' mind was awhirl with confusion, as he realized that he was still holding the butt of his gun to his shoulder. Immediately, he lowered it and slung the weapon back over his shoulder. He called back, holding his own hands up in reassurance, "I did not mean to frighten you; indeed, I did not even know you were there."

She nodded and said, "I was hiding and was not aware of your presence in this field, either, until you shot at me." She glared at him, her dark eyes flashing and he gasped in disbelief that she could think that he would have fired on her.

"What? I did not shoot at you!" He gestured past her, to where the wounded goose could still be heard struggling. "I am here hunting for my supper only and did not think that there was another soul in this field."

Look for The Path: Tales From a Revolution - Rhode-Island at your favorite booksellers.

Made in the USA
Columbia, SC
15 November 2021

48977016R00136